TEMPTING TWO

SCANDALOUS BALLROOM ENCOUNTERS BOOK 3

VICTORIA VALE

PROLOGUE

*P*enelope Hunt's hands shook violently, despite the determined clasp of her fingers. Her knuckles had gone white, and her face had likely drained of all color, as well. Despite the crackling fire in the inn's hearth, cold shrouded her, as if her blood had been replaced with ice water.

Staring down at the rumpled bit of parchment at her feet, her eyes began to water, causing her vision to blur. It didn't matter; she'd read the words eight times after discovering the letter resting on the pillow beside her in Colin's place. The first reading had caused a fissure deep within her heart, and each rereading had only caused that crevice to grow, leaving a resounding ache which seemed to echo to the furthest reaches of her body.

Upon arriving at the inn last night, she had been filled with happiness and hope. At the foot of the bed rested her portmanteau, in which a white muslin morning dress—her best one with the French lace and pearls bedecking the bodice—had been stored. A matching hat with pink roses pinned along the brim, and short, white lace gloves completed the get-up, along with the pearls her stepfather had given her on her sixteenth birthday. A modest, yet beautiful wedding ensemble she had thought to wear today.

A second travelling dress lay in the bag as well, a deep mauve carriage gown that she'd always thought made her look older than her years. The perfect frock for a newly married woman.

Never had she imagined she would return to London alone and unmarried. After all, when a girl ran off to Gretna Green in the dead of night, she typically returned home a married woman. Yet, she would return without her virginity, her dignity, or the expected husband. There would be nothing to show for one night of poor judgment but a paltry sheet of paper upon which Colin's hastily scrawled words spelled out Penelope's worst fear.

A hot tear escaped the corner of one eye, scorching a path down her cheek toward her jaw. Her chin began to tremble, and try as she might, she could not bring it under control. With a loud sniffle, she dashed at her tears, anger making her motions jerky and unrefined. Penelope despised weakness and had never abided simpering, weepy females. How was it that Colin Worthing possessed the power to turn her into just the sort of woman she hated?

Deciding she didn't care, since no one was here to see her anyway, she buried her face in her hands, crumpling Colin's letter and weeping upon the paper. Her chest heaved with sobs, and a sound that very much reminded her of a wounded horse echoed from the walls around her.

It was a wonder she heard the angry bellow of a man's voice and the pounding of booted feet upon the steps before the door flew open to reveal her stepfather. A large man—both tall and broad—with limbs like tree trunks, he made quite an imposing sight in his many-caped greatcoat and beaver hat, his hair a sodden, bedraggled tangle from the rain.

She shot to her feet, clutching the wrinkled, damp slip of paper to her breast. Even knowing she must look a fright, she did nothing to set her tousled hair, rumpled nightgown, or blotchy, wet face to rights. While the Marquis of Hartford had not sired her, he had helped her mother raise her after her own father had died when she had been only seven years old. For all intents and purposes, the man was her papa, and just then, she knew he saw and felt her pain. He knew, without her having to tell him, that everything had gone wrong.

Closing the door swiftly behind him, he held his arms out to her.

"Oh, dearest," he murmured.

Hurtling across the space between them, she fell into his arms, not bothering to stifle her noisy sobs. Patting her back, he held her in silence until the spasms in her chest stilled, and her sobs had quieted to soft groans interspersed with hiccups.

"Where is he?" Hartford asked, his voice clipped and brusque.

Penelope gazed up at him, her heart sinking at the expression of fury on his face. She had never seen the lines upon his brow look so deep. Or the corners of his mouth draw down so far.

"He is gone, Papa. He's not coming back."

Handing him the letter, she stood back and tried to collect herself. His brown eyes darted back and forth as he scanned the note, darkening when he came to the end. His large, meaty hand closed around the paper, crumpling it into a ball.

"That bastard. That spoiled, arrogant little ingrate!"

She shuddered when his voice thundered from the rafters. Even though he would never harm her, his anger frightened her. If she'd ever had any doubt of Hartford's love for her, this moment would have eased them. His fury was all on her behalf.

"Come, get dressed. We've a long ride back to London. I am going to leave you with your mother, who has been worried sick since we found your note telling us where you'd gone. Then, I have an afternoon call to make. Lord Worthing and I have much to discuss."

Viscount Worthing, Colin's father, would be furious with his son for what he had done. After all, even third sons were held to a gentlemanly code of conduct. Seducing young debutantes with promises of marriage and deflowering them before leaving them cold was simply not done.

Penelope knew what would happen if the two men met to discuss what had occurred in this room. Colin would be dragged to Hartford House by his collar with the marquis' pistol trained at his back. A quiet wedding would follow, after which they would be secreted away on a trip to some country estate under the pretense of a honeymoon trip. In truth, they would be hiding out to escape the gossip sure to follow their rather hasty nuptials.

Though no one should be surprised if they wed. After all, Colin had publicly courted her all season. If anything, that fact only made his betrayal all the more nefarious. It wasn't as if he had made his despicable intentions known from the start. He'd been the perfect gentleman—kissing her hand, bringing her flowers, charming her parents. Only in private had he stolen a few chaste kisses and intimate caresses. She'd only allowed it because she loved him, and had thought he loved her back.

It had all been a game to him, she realized. He had never loved her, only sought to earn her trust so that he could deflower her. Penelope's mother had warned her of such men before the start of her first Season, but she had never believed Colin could be capable of such behavior.

"No!" she exclaimed. "Please, do not go to Colin's father. I couldn't bear it!"

Hartford's brow furrowed in consternation. "But, Penny, if I don't go—"

"Then Colin would have ruined me without having to pay the price for his indiscretion. Yes, Papa, I know."

"He ... he ... assaulted you."

Sighing, she dried the last of her tears. Like her mother, she'd always possessed the uncanny ability to pick up and move on after a crisis. It was how they'd gotten by after her father's death. It would be the way she healed from this wound, as well.

"No, he did not. Colin might have seduced me, but I wanted to be seduced. I thought myself in love with him, but I realize now that I was foolish and indiscreet. I thought I wanted to marry him, but I could never trust my body, mind, and heart to a man who would sneak away like a coward in the middle of the night and leave nothing but a note behind. I would despise him, and I am certain he would abhor me. Neither of us would want this marriage, and no good could come from forcing it."

A sound of frustration emitted from the back of his throat, and he pressed a large hand against his brow, attempting to smooth the wrinkles with this thumb and forefinger.

"You do realize there will be gossip? Your abigail found the note you left, and you know how servants talk. People may come to know. Your chances of making a good match after this will be slim."

Raising her chin, she squared her shoulders. "That is quite all right. I've decided that I rather dislike the business of courting and shopping for a husband on the Marriage Mart. It's all intrigues ... smoke and mirrors. Lies. I want no part in it, or any man who would think me ruined just because of one indiscretion. Besides, perhaps *I* do not want a ruined man who has spread his seed from here to Bath."

Chuckling, the marquis took her shoulders in a firm but gentle grip. "You have always been an infuriatingly independent woman, as well as reasonable and level-headed. Of course, you know your mother will insist."

"Tell her you tried, but Colin and Lord Worthing would not be swayed. Tell her what you must, but please do not force me to marry him. It would ruin me ... truly ruin me."

Nodding, he released her. "Very well. You know I would do anything to make you and your mother happy. She might not like it at first, but in time, we will all forget this ever happened."

They both knew he attempted to be optimistic, but Penelope said nothing. She did not tell him that she planned to do just the opposite. Forgetting what Colin had done would be a mistake, but remembering ... ah, remembering would protect her. No man would ever use or manipulate her again, that was certain.

"I will wait for you downstairs in the dining room," the marquis declared, striding for the door. "I hope the food here is decent so we can have a meal before setting off for home."

"I'll be down in a moment," she promised, closing the door behind him.

Taking her time, Penelope changed from her nightgown and into her traveling clothes. As she unbuttoned the front of the prim, white garment, she tried not to think about Colin's deft fingers performing the same action the night before, or his lips following the opening vee as the two sides fell apart to reveal her breasts. Swiftly stuffing the gown into her portmanteau, she finished dressing, ensuring she portrayed the perfect image of a highborn lady before stepping from the room.

Hands covered with gloves, hat held between her fingers, and every strand of hair in place, she felt prepared to face the world once more. Just before leaving, she took once last look back. Spying the wrinkled note where her stepfather had left it, she went back to retrieve it. Without a second thought, she placed it, along with the rumpled nightgown, inside her bag.

"Thank you, Colin," she murmured as she strode toward the stairs, "for a most valuable lesson."

CHAPTER 1

As his coach rolled to a halt before the front steps of one of the largest and most grandiose townhouses on Grosvenor Square, Colin Worthing gazed through the vehicle's window and mused over how little London had changed. The warmth of spring had descended, and with it, the pomp and tradition marking the start of the Season. Three grand fêtes had been planned for the evening, and tomorrow afternoon, every drawing room in the city would fill with the usual gossip. Whose ball had been the grandest? What lady had worn the most scandalous gown? Which debutantes had the most beauty and promise? How many of the *ton*'s confirmed bachelors would find themselves snared in the marriage trap?

Very little had changed in the three years since his escape from London, yet everything seemed different. He felt like a stranger here, an imposter. The man who'd returned home from Belgium did not resemble the young rake who had left, making it difficult to take part in the usual revelry and decadent laziness that marked the lifestyles of England's upper crust.

There had been a time he would have reveled in the decadence of it. Using an evening like this one as an opportunity to scour the ballroom for potential bedmates. Gaming hells, brothels, gambling and insane quantities of spirits … all a part of his past. Pouring his inebriated self into bed at dawn and sleeping off the debaucheries of the night before no longer appealed. His reputation had awaited him upon his return, like some mantle to be donned. It was only one of the reasons he had spent so much time closeted away at home after returning home—the second being the injury to his leg.

Still, life must go on, and he could no longer live in the past. And so, he had forced himself to get dressed and emerge from his family's townhouse for the first time since arriving in the city several months past. The time had come for him to surface from the shadows and move out from under the fog he'd been living beneath since Waterloo. His days in the army had ended, which meant the next phase of his life must begin.

Marriage. Children. Stability. They had become more necessary now than ever, but even so, he found he wanted them for himself. And if he *had* to marry and begin a family, there existed only one woman he wanted to do it with.

Lady Penelope Hunt.

A knot of apprehension tightened in his gut at the thought of the girl he had ruined three years prior. Not a day passed that she did not invade his thoughts. He had imagined the moment he would see her again so many times, in so many different ways, that he really ought to have been prepared for anything. Despite that, he found himself battling a case of nerves unlike any he'd ever experienced.

He had gleaned as much information about her as he could from the privacy of his family's townhome, where he'd resided since returning to London. She remained unwed, which he could only take as a sign from God that his timing couldn't have been better. If she had not wed in all this time, perhaps he still had a chance with her. If she had decided she'd rather see him publicly hanged rather than marry him, well … there was always groveling.

Determination squared his jaw as the door of the coach swung open to reveal his footman, who swiftly lowered the step for him. Clutching the gilded walking stick that he carried as much out of necessity as he did for style, Colin descended from the conveyance.

Warmth and light spilled out onto the steps through the open front door, inviting him into the foyer. As he was led to the ballroom, he steeled himself for a night of pity and hero worship—an inevitable circumstance of having survived Waterloo. He supposed as a younger man, he might have reveled in the attention, even using it to gain entrance into the bedrooms of many willing women. However, if he'd learned anything during his time in the army, it was that the men who bragged about their heroics in public were actually the biggest cowards on the battlefield. Even if he did want to speak of what he'd seen and done while at war, he would not disrespect the memory of the friends he'd lost by bragging. Being one of the few in his regiment to make it home did not feel like much of an accomplishment.

The receiving line did not stretch very long, and Colin soon found himself bowing to the Duke and Duchess of Avonleah. One of the things that had changed during his absence proved to be the transformation of Lord Camden Rycroft from libertine to devoted husband and father. The difference made itself evident in the duke's countenance—his normally heavy-lidded air of affected boredom now replaced by one of genuine openness and warmth. It gave Colin hope for his own redemption.

"Captain Worthing," Avonleah exclaimed, seeming surprised to see him. "I'd heard you were in town months ago. It is good to clap eyes on you at last. May I present to you my wife, Lady Margaret Rycroft, Duchess of Avonleah."

Taking the lady's hand, Colin bowed over it and kissed the air just above it. "Your Grace. Rumors of the beauty who tamed the wild duke reached us all the way to Belgium. I am happy to find that you have more than lived up to the tales of your loveliness."

"Now, that is more than enough," the duke teased, smoothly retrieving her hand from Colin's. "Keep an eye on this one, darling. In my days as a rake, there existed only one man who could match me, and you are looking at him."

Colin joined the duchess in a laugh, leaning a bit on his cane. Standing still for too long aggravated his injured leg.

"I've hung my rake's hat up for good, I'm afraid," he said. "I hope the end of the Season will see me happily wed."

Clapping his shoulder, the duke grinned. "Good show, Captain. Enjoy the evening."

Seeing that the receiving line had come to a standstill behind him, he bid the duke and duchess good evening and entered the ballroom. Halting at the top of the curving staircase leading down into the crush, he presented his card and waited to be announced.

"Captain Colin Worthing!"

Descending the curved staircase, he became aware that hundreds of pairs of eyes followed his progress. Squaring his shoulders, he let his hand skim the balustrade and tried not too lean too hard upon his walking stick. The moment someone noticed his limp, the pity ensued.

Returning the gazes of those staring outright without even trying to hide their curiosity, he entered the crush. Voices called out to him, hands found their way into his, pleasantries were exchanged. It all passed him by in a blur of formalities while he searched the ballroom for the only face he cared to see.

He had come fashionably late, and if he knew Penelope, she would already have arrived. She hated scrutiny, and would have wanted to arrive before people began paying attention to who came and went.

In a sea of milky blondes and drab brunettes, he sought out the beacon of her auburn locks. She must be here—he had it on good authority her presence would be expected.

"Ah, there you are," said a voice from his side. "I had begun to think you wouldn't show."

He turned to find Lord Edmond Ingham, future Earl of Kesbridge and his best friend since Eton, smiling down at him. Taller than Colin and wiry, he reeked of old money. Refined, well-dressed, educated, and in line to inherit, the first son of an earl holding the courtesy title of viscount ... Edmond seemed to own the world. Only Colin knew the dire straits his father had placed their family in. Gambling debts had chipped away at the family fortune until very little of it remained.

Still, Edmond had turned out for this evening's ball in grand style, his outer appearance belying the truth of his dismal circumstances.

"Not show?" Colin mimicked, raising an eyebrow. "And miss the chance to watch you all make fools of yourself trying to nab the prettiest or wealthiest chits? Never."

Edmond grimaced, gaze darting about the ballroom. "There aren't many prospects on the pretty end this year, I'm afraid. Though we both know for me it does not matter. Money wins over beauty when you're months away from debtors' prison."

He scoffed. "They don't throw earls or viscounts into debtors' prison. They simply refuse to extend you more credit and embarrass you. Besides, you are heir to an old title, and you're almost as good-looking as me. Find a girl to wed, do it quickly, and use her dowry to set things right."

"The old man will only piss it all away again. I wish he would do me the great honor of dying."

Knowing how his friend only jested and loved his father despite his faults, Colin laughed and pounded him on the shoulder.

"Pray hard enough, and a runaway carriage or temperamental horse might solve all your problems."

Edmond procured two tumblers of champagne from a passing footman and gave one to Colin. Between sips, he continued scanning the ballroom—undoubtedly plotting this best strategy for wife-hunting.

"What of you?" he murmured. "Won't you be joining the bloodhounds in the hunt? I seem to recall you left your bed for the purpose of finding a bride."

"Correction," Colin replied. "I left my bed in favor of the chaise longue in the yellow drawing room. I left the chaise in favor of coming here tonight, but there will be no hunt. I already know who I'm going to marry."

Edmond groaned. "Not this again. Colin, I have been your friend since we were in leading strings, which is why I feel I am most qualified to remind you of reality. She is never going to marry you. In fact, if you attempt to approach her, you'll be fortunate to walk away with all your teeth."

He was right, dash it all, but Colin wasn't ready to admit defeat just yet.

"Have you seen her? I have to at least try."

Craning his neck, Edmond searched the room with all the discretion of an ostrich.

"Right, no need to be inconspicuous about it," Colin muttered.

"You cannot afford to be subtle. An outright assault is your best strategy, and even then, it's a lost cause. Perhaps begging will increase your odds, but not by much. Ah, there she is."

Forgetting discretion, he whipped his head in the same direction Edmond gazed to find her. His fingers clenched around the head of his walking stick, and his throat constricted at the sight of her.

Everything about her was just as he remembered. The smooth, alabaster skin, and lustrous auburn locks with matching eyelashes lowered demurely toward high cheekbones. The plump lips just begging to be kissed.

And yet, everything about her had changed. As she talked and laugh with a group mostly made up of men, Penelope appeared like a queen holding court. Shoulders squared, head high, mouth curved into a smile that was downright sensual. Beneath her pristine ivory gown, her body appeared to have blossomed. The breasts he had palmed and teased with his tongue appeared fuller and more decadent, her hips seeming to have followed suit. She laughed, and the throaty timbre of it slammed into him, causing his blood to heat. His cock stirred at the sound.

"Christ," he murmured, handing his empty tumbler off to one footman and snatching a full glass from another.

Edmond chuckled as he downed the entire thing in one swallow.

"Three years has done a lot for our Penelope. She was a pretty thing when she came out, but now … she can hardly keep the men away."

"Yet, she remains unmarried."

Edmond snorted. "It hasn't been for lack of offers. Many a man has tried, and all have failed."

"What is she waiting for?" he murmured.

You.

Possible, but not likely. Colin had hurt her in the worst way, and he would be an idiot to think she still cared anything about him.

However, if there existed even the slightest possibility, he would pursue her until she realized the truth. He had always loved her, even if his behavior indicated otherwise. Now, he would prove it.

"Well, there she is," Edmond said. "Go get her."

He shook his head. "Not yet. I need to know how she feels after all this time first, and I cannot do that in front of three hundred people."

Glancing from him to Penelope and back again, Edmond rubbed his smooth chin.

"Hmmm, perhaps I can do something about that."

"Christ, Ed, this isn't our first Season. We are beyond the days of ballroom intrigues and covert messages."

"You might be, but I'm not. I do not plan to be until I have wed, either. I signed her card for the first quadrille. While we dance, I shall simply mention that you are here tonight—"

"As if she doesn't know," Colin interposed. "The entire ballroom is filled with talk of who is here, who isn't, and why it matters."

"Precisely. I'm not an idiot. Mentioning your presence will simply earn a reaction from her. Then, depending on her response, I might be able to talk her into meeting you in the garden for a tête-à-tête."

"I did not want to do things this way. All the secrecy and intrigue … it is how we did things last time, and look how it ended."

"Before all the secrecy and intrigue, you had the chance to do things the right way, publicly. You ruined it like the jackanapes you are."

He glared at Edmond. "I say, whose side are you on?"

"Yours, naturally. But the length of our friendship means I can tell you the truth. You stand little chance with her now."

"You're right, of course. Still, I must try."

"Of course you must. Never let it be said that Captain Worthing shies away from a challenge. Very well, I shall endeavor to convince her to meet you. If she agrees, I will give the usual signal."

Ah, the signal, a hand through the hair and a glance at his watch—a remnant of their old days on the prowl.

Taking up yet another glass of champagne, Colin nodded. "I'll be waiting."

Half the people occupying this ballroom with Penelope did so on the pretense of finding a mate. The evidence of that made itself apparent in the behavior of said persons—pleasant courtesies murmured as names were scrawled onto dance cards, plenty of blushing and hiding behind fans, and veiled innuendo.

Ah, the start of the Season. All the youngest chits would be brought out, and those who had not fared well last year or the year before would make a valiant go at it again.

As for Penelope … well, she embarked upon her fourth Season and remained husbandless. However, unlike other women her age, she did not lament her lack of beau. In fact, as she neared her twenty-fifth birthday, she rather enjoyed her current position— free of attachment. Thirty days from now, she would inherit her own dowry. The money had been left by her father, who had set it aside the moment the physician informed him his wife had birthed a girl. Because the marquis loved her as much as he did Penelope's mother, he had doubled the amount after becoming her stepfather.

Upon reaching her majority, Penelope would be richer than many of her male peers, freeing her to live life as she pleased. The only thing that would make this Season all the more exciting would be finding someone to enjoy a discreet affair with. After her disastrous first Season, she had given up the husband hunt in favor of temporary arrangements. She had taken lovers the past two seasons, and had every intention of repeating the experience.

Just the thought of indulging in an amorous relationship again made the surface of her skin tingle. It caused a wide smile to spread across her face between sips of champagne, and for her to laugh because the excitement became too much to contain. This approach to the Season appealed to her so much more than the stiff conversations and endless dances with boring men who wished to wed her. While she might interact with a few just to keep up pretenses, it had become widely known that she sat on the shelf, which was where she intended to remain. Every man who had asked for her hand after Colin had been turned down. If anyone were keeping score—which she did not doubt as betting books in men's club all over London were filled with the silliest wagers—their card might read: Lady Penelope Hunt 4, Bachelors of London 0.

Four proposals, all of which she'd turned down, much to her mother's astonishment. The marquis, of course, understood the reasons for her decisions and supported them. A doting papa, he seemed all too happy to send each suitor packing once Penelope had refused him.

The only questioned remained who her chosen lover would be. She had begun perusing the men in the room the moment she'd arrived. A few of her prospects had signed her dance card, giving her ample opportunity for conversation. Since this was her third year at it, she had become quite adept at selecting the perfect men—careful to steer clear of the marriage hopefuls, or those with too rakish a reputation. Widowers, confirmed bachelors, men avoiding the marriage noose just like her ... these were the sorts of men she could depend upon to prove good company in and out of bed, but not give her the pox or treat her poorly.

"Lady Penelope?"

The sound of a man's voice broke her out of her reverie, and she found herself in Lord Edmond Ingham's illustrious presence.

Christ, the man was beautiful. Tall and slender with broad shoulders, hair like midnight sweeping his brow. Vibrant green eyes hooded by black brows might have been intimidating if not for the pleasant twinkle found there. Edmond appeared a man constantly at ease and always laughing. Penelope admired a sense of humor. Aside from that, he seemed intelligent, though one might notice his looks and humor before realizing the man was sharp as a nail.

He had not been on her original list, but just then, as he extended his hand to her with a smile, he found himself there.

"I've come to claim you."

A shudder wracked her at his words, wrapped in his velvety voice. Deep. Resonant. Almost like a cat's purr … a jungle cat.

However, she did not intend to be his prey. She preferred to do the stalking.

Raising an eyebrow, she placed a hand in his. "Claim me? My lord, don't you think you ought to bring me champagne first?"

A flicker of surprise at her boldness lit in his gaze before he laughed. She'd caught him off guard. Good.

He cleared his throat. "Erm, for the quadrille. I've come to claim you for our dance."

Feigning a disappointed pout, she allowed him to lead her toward the dance floor, where others prepared for the quadrille to begin.

"Well, I suppose a dance will do to start. Lead the way, if you please."

His white-gloved hand was large, strong. The fingers gripping hers seemed sure and steady. She would wager he knew how to do a great many things with those hands.

"You look lovely this evening," he murmured as they took their positions in a circle consisting of four couples.

"And you, most dashing, my lord. A new coat?"

He smirked, and the music began. After bowing to the woman at his left, he turned and bowed to her, while she curtsied to the man at her right first, then him.

"You notice such things?" he murmured.

Their bouncy steps took them past each other, first in one direction, then the other.

"A lady always does. It has the stiffness of new fabric, and the fit of a garment recently sewn. You cut quite an impressive figure in it."

A long pause in their conversation ensued as Edmond took his turn performing steps in the center of the circle with the woman across from him. Then it became time for her and the gentleman across from her to join. All the while, his gaze snuck to her, though his feet remained sure, his steps impeccable.

His smirk transformed into a smile when they joined hands and frolicked in a tight circle. "Thank you, but ... well, shouldn't I be the one to lavish *you* with compliments?"

She laughed. "Only if you feel threatened at the prospect of reversed roles. Besides, I'd much rather be complimented on something more substantial than my looks."

Edmond's vibrant eyes followed her as she joined the other three ladies in the center of the circle. Joining her hand to theirs, she followed them in a circle, first in one direction, then the other, a spring in her step as she giggled and gave him a wide smile.

They came together again, dancing close.

One of his dark eyebrows rose toward his hairline. "Fascinating."

"Me, my lord?" she panted from between short breaths.

A moment of rest came while another couple met in the center to dance. He turned his head toward her.

"Yes, you. It is easy to see why Colin is so enamored."

Annoyance caused her spine to go rigid, her jaw to clench.

"My lord, I am not at all interested in the inner workings of Captain Worthing's mind."

He nodded. "Fair enough. However, I've been led to believe there remains unfinished business between you."

She scoffed, hoping to disguise the tremor in her voice and the fact that the mention of Colin had thrown her off guard. How could she have forgotten the two were best friends?

"I hardly see how it's any of your business, my lord."

"It wouldn't be if not for Colin. As his best friend, it falls to me to warn him that he stands an ice cube's chance in Hell with you." He shrugged with an exaggerated motion. "Alas, the stubborn idiot will hear those words from no one but you."

Despite herself, she snickered. "He always was stubborn."

"And an idiot," he added, lips quivering with contained laughter. "Don't forget that part."

They joined together for the final steps of the dance, their gazes locked.

"So, you're here as a messenger. Not because you want to be?"

He licked his lips and lowered his voice. "Don't be silly. Dancing with you has been the highlight of my evening. Colin's message is irrelevant when compared to that."

Her pulse thumped, and she bit back a sigh. Edmond Ingham did not know it, but he had just secured the top place on her list of prospective lovers for the Season. The promise of what his hands could be capable of proved too delicious to ignore.

"Please, Miss Hunt," he continued as the music ended. "Meet him in the garden and hear him out … for the sake of my own sanity."

She curtsied to him while he bowed, then he took her hand to guide her from the dance floor.

"You wish for me to speak with Colin … as a favor to you?"

Tucking her hand into the crook of his arm, he patted it, giving her another one of his tremor-inducing smiles.

"I would be forever in your debt."

Surely, a short conversation with Colin would not be so bad. After all, the elephant in the room should be addressed. He must be made to understand that what he'd done to her meant nothing now. In fact, she'd become a stronger woman for it. Showing him that and walking away would be so deliciously fun.

"Very well, my lord. I will speak to him, if for no other reason than having you in my debt is a most alluring prospect."

Releasing her once they'd cleared the dance floor, he turned to face her, hands clasped behind his back.

"I can hardly wait for you to collect," he murmured with a wink.

Without responding, she offered her hand, never breaking his gaze as he raised it to his lips and kissed it.

"Until then, my lord," she murmured, turning to saunter off.

Without glancing back, she could feel his stare on her. Yes, he would make a most satisfactory lover. The only thing left to do before pursuing the liaison was put a certain rogue captain in his place.

Spying his brilliant scarlet coat and the beacon of his golden head near the garden doors, she followed, determined to be finished with Colin Worthing once and for all.

CHAPTER 2

olin sat on a stone bench in Avonleah's garden, his walking stick propped beside him. Elbows braced on his knees, he watched the open double doors of the ballroom for any sign of Penelope. He clenched his hands together to stop them from trembling and drew in a deep breath. In the years since he'd last encountered her, he'd imagined this moment in so many ways. While some of those fantasies bordered on absurd, he held out hope that she still felt something for him, even after what he'd done. He did not expect her to fall into his arms, but if she did not slap him on sight, it would give him something to build on.

She materialized at the doors, her steps purposeful as she drew near. The moonlight framed her, setting her gown and alabaster skin aglow, causing the red hues of her hair to gleam.

Seeing her this way reminded him of the night he'd come for her, waiting with a horse in carriage to secret her away from Gretna Green. A young scapegrace with a slew of shameful deeds behind him, Colin had taken one look at the young girl he loved, and realized he would never be good enough for her. The youth in that fresh face, the innocence in her gaze, the blind truth with which she allowed him to take her away, expecting to return a married woman—they all served to remind him that she was everything he was not. He'd been determined to prove to himself that he could deserve her, that her innocence, sweetness, and love for him could redeem him.

Yet, in the end, he'd ruined everything. His path toward redemption had taken him down a longer, harder road, but he wasn't finished yet. Seeing her again reminded him of how little he deserved her, yet this time he wouldn't run from that fact. He would face the truth, then fight to earn her.

Grasping his walking stick, he used it to hoist himself to his feet, ignoring the twinge of pain in his leg caused by long hours spent standing. Her scent reached him when she paused before him, sweet and floral.

"Penny," he murmured, allowing his gaze to trace the lines and planes of her face freely.

She tilted her chin and met his gaze with boldness. "*Lady* Penelope, if you please, or just Penelope, if you insist. I no longer answer to Penny."

He fought back a frown. Her tone had grown cold, her insistence on formality not like the woman he'd known.

What did you expect, you clodpole?

"Penelope," he amended. "You look … well."

She raised her eyebrows and gave a dry chuckle. "Surely, you did not send for me so we could discuss my health."

Taking a step toward her, he reached out to grasp her chin. She did not resist when he lifted it, his thumb tracing the line of her lower lip. Her gaze remained locked with his, challenging, defiant.

"I did not mean 'well' in that way. In fact, I should have chosen my words better. Though none of them would do you justice, but I'll try. Beautiful, Penelope. You look more beautiful than I remember."

Scoffing, she pulled away from his touch, brushing past him. "I see some things never change. You're still the silver-tongued flatterer you always were."

Turning to follow, he limped while leaning on his cane, struggling to keep up with her.

"Many things have changed about me. I'd like the chance to prove that to you."

Entering the hedgerow maze, she shook her head, throwing up her hands with a snort. "And now, you begin with the lies! I wondered how long it would take."

Gritting his teeth, he followed, grunting as his thigh began to throb. "I understand you might be angry—"

Pausing suddenly, she swiveled to face him, bringing him up short. "Angry? On the contrary, Colin. I feel nothing toward you. Anger, least of all."

The fists balled up at her sides told a different story, but he chose not to point that out.

"I just wanted a chance to clear the air between us," he said. "We never spoke again after that night at the inn."

She pursed her lips. "Yes, well, one can hardly engage in a conversation with someone as they go running back to their father with their tail tucked between their legs now, can they?"

"Point taken," he replied. "I know I have no right to ask this, but I just ... please let me explain."

Clasping her hands in front of her, she cleared her throat. "Very well. I am listening, Colin."

Her coldness had begun to take its toll, causing a pit of despair to open in his gut. However, he wasn't ready to concede defeat just yet.

"When I asked you to marry me, the offer was sincere. My love for you was real."

Her expression remained neutral, as if his words had no impact. He cleared his throat and soldiered on.

"We might be wed now if I weren't such a coward. You see, that night after we ... after we made love ... I laid in that bed while you slept beside me, and felt terror. I'd never loved anyone before, Penelope. It was intense, and all-consuming, and it frightened me. Before you, I was concerned only with burying my cock in as many women as I could, thinking it would turn me into some sort of hero—a rake for all the other idiots to look up to and crown as their king. It was all about conquest and bragging rights, and I'd never felt anything real … until I met you. You breathed life into me, and you made me want to be a better person. For a time, it seemed to work. I felt as if I were ready to commit to being your husband, to being a good man. But, fear crept in and I allowed it to drive my actions. I didn't understand true love— not the way I should have to be a good husband to anyone. I was too young and inexperienced to understand it, so I ran. I regret what I did, and not a day passes me by when I do not think of it and feel shame."

When he fell silent, she took a deep, noisy breath, nostrils flaring as she exhaled. "How long did it take you to experience this shame, Colin? Was it after you'd gotten dressed and left the inn? Or perhaps during the long ride from Gretna Green back to London? Oh, I know … maybe it was as you stood before your father, telling him what you had done and begging him to clean up your mess. No, but it could not have been then, because you still accepted the commission he purchased for you and left. So, tell me, Colin. When did the guilt over-whelm you?"

He lowered his gaze, determined to weather this first encounter without losing faith. Now was her opportunity to say to him every-thing she'd never gotten to say.

"I do not expect you to believe me," he replied. "If war has taught me anything, it's that life has no guarantees. I faced death in Belgium, and realized I had so many regrets. You stood foremost in my mind. I was given a second chance at life, even though I did not deserve it. It opened my eyes to the other wrongs I needed to right in my life."

"So you thought to soothe your conscience, so that you might return to society and resume your life guilt-free?"

"No, it's not that, Penelope—"

"Allow me to spare you the trouble, Colin. Apology accepted. I forgive you. In fact, I forgave you years ago, so that *I* could move on with *my* life. Now, kindly go away and never attempt to speak to me again."

She moved to walk past him, but he was unwilling to let her get away. Grasping her arm, he halted her, pulling her against him.

"I faced many options after Waterloo, many of which involved avoiding London and you. I could have outrun it all if I'd wished. I chose to come back for one reason, and it has nothing to do with my conscience. It's you, Penny. I came for you. I love—"

"Don't!" she growled, dislodging her arm from his hold. "Don't you dare say those words to me. They mean nothing falling from your lips … not anymore."

He nodded. "You're right. I've given you no reason to trust me. That's why I want the chance to earn it, the right way this time."

Throwing all his pride aside, he fell to one knee before her, reaching for one of her hands.

"Please, Penny. I'll do anything. Give me a chance to show you my words are true."

Staring down at him, her gaze remained cool. "*Penelope.*"

He nodded. "Right, sorry. Old habits and all that. Penelope, please."

For a moment, she simply gazed down at him in silence, her expression inscrutable. Colin held his breath, waiting for her to either tear his heart to shreds, or buoy it with her next words.

"The fact is," she said, reaching down to stroke his hair. "I never actually loved you, Colin. I realized after you left that I was only a young girl who allowed lust and infatuation to cloud her judgement. I wanted to fuck someone, and you wanted my virginity. We both got what we wanted."

He creased his brow, shaking his head. "I don't believe you. No one can fake emotion like that. I saw it in your eyes."

Curling her upper lip, she scoffed. "And now? What do you see, Colin?"

"A woman who is far stronger than I ever gave her credit for. One who will never allow anyone to come close to her again, and all because of what I did."

She rolled her eyes. "Not everything is about you. I am this way because I want to be. I'm unwed because I enjoy my independence, and I do not have time for the games and intrigue that accompany the courting ritual. This is who I am, and I like things this way. If I ever did love you, that feeling is gone."

Raising an eyebrow, he reached for one of her ankles, stroking up her stockinged calf. "And what of lust? That emotion is much harder to put aside, isn't it?"

Despite the fact that she shuddered, Penelope remained stoic. "Nonsense. I am perfectly capable of putting lust aside."

He felt his lips twisting into a smirk as he lifted her foot, resting it on his thigh. His leg screamed in protest against his position, but he ignored it, concentrating on the smooth silk stocking at his fingertips and the shapely leg it encased.

"Poppycock," he murmured. "I know you, Penelope. I can hear your breath growing uneven, and see the rise and fall of your breasts. You aren't as unaffected by me as you'd like to pretend."

She did not respond. Neither did she pull away as his hand skimmed higher, encountering the leg of her pantaloons. Edging his fingers beneath the fabric, he stroked bare skin.

Leaning forward, he rested his head against her middle, drawing slow circles on her inner thigh.

"Your skin is just like I remember. So soft. I wonder, would you still moan if I did this?"

She shuddered, muffling a moan when he found an especially sensitive spot near the crease where her thigh met her pelvis.

"There," he whispered, pressing a kiss against her belly through the fabric of her gown. "I remember. Do you? I would trace that spot with my tongue, then nibble on the inside of your thigh. God, I remember you tasting so good. I could feast on you for hours."

Penelope whimpered, teetering on one foot, then steadied herself by gripping his shoulder.

"I do remember your tongue being good for a bit more than lying."

He chuckled. "We were good together. Don't you remember?

When we made love, it was unlike anything I've ever known. We could have that again."

Grasping his hair, she gave it a gentle but firm tug, tilting his head back to meet his gaze. Her lips curved into a coy smirk that sent blood rushing straight to his groin. His cock strained against the front of his breeches, begging for entrance to her body.

"You're right," she whispered. "We were good together. I do want that again. Here. Now."

A tremor rolled down his spine, his mouth watering at the prospect of being with her again. He stood, eagerness making his movements less than graceful as he reached for her.

Shaking her head, she pressed a hand to his chest, urging him back downward. Her eyes twinkled with mischief as she gave him a sensual smile.

"No, Colin. Back on your knees."

Her command caused his erection to grow even more painful. He reached down to apply pressure to the throbbing organ, hoping to ease the ache until he could bury himself in her.

As he obeyed the order, he found himself intrigued by the woman he thought he'd known. The sweet, shy girl she'd been before was nothing like the bold vixen who stood before him, commanding him to kneel.

He liked it.

CHAPTER 3

Penelope took her time lifting her skirts, enjoying the way Colin's eyes darkened in reaction. She had underestimated the impact his presence would have on her. While anger remained ever-present, another feeling had caught her off-guard.

Desire.

No amount of anger could wipe away her attraction to him. It had been a long winter, and she was starved for release. Since Colin already knelt before her, she saw no reason to deny him the privilege of pleasuring her. He obviously wanted it, his hand skimming her stockings, gliding up over her ankles and calves, gripping with light but firm pressure. His fingers sank deeper as he moved higher, his thumb massaging her inner thighs. Beneath dark blond brows, his sapphire-blue eyes crackled with electricity as he stared up at her, his hunger unmistakable.

She shuddered, her breath growing harsher as he found the seam between her lower lips, tracing it with his fingertip. Her sheath contracted, the deep need for penetration causing a slow pulsation to grow and build within her.

His hands gripped her hips, fingers sinking into the plump cheeks of her arse, then moved higher to the waistband of her drawers. Leaning forward, he took the ribbon between his teeth and yanked, his breath tickling the naked skin of her lower belly. The drawers loosened, then fell to her ankles.

Urging her to sit on the bench he'd just occupied, he remained in his subservient position. She leaned back against the back of the bench, lifting her legs so he could remove her drawers. He slid his hands beneath her, gripping her buttocks and moving her forward until she slouched, her hips level with the edge of the seat.

Resting his cheek against the inside of her thigh, he sighed—it tickled the curls covering her mons, sending a shiver up her spine.

"God, I've missed you, Penny," he whispered.

She bit her lip to keep from responding. All she wanted was for him to give her pleasure—not call her Penny, or tell her how he felt. She needed him to chase away the longing in her gut by fulfilling her baser needs. Those were the only desires that mattered to her right now.

His thumb delved between her nether lips, caressing the soft inner folds. She whimpered, spreading her legs wider and raising her hips. Massaging in slow circles, he found her pearl. He teased the bud, coaxing wetness from her core in response.

The old Penelope might have lain still in submission, allowing him to pleasure her on his terms. However, she'd learned a lot about herself, one of those things being that she preferred dominance.

Reaching down, she grasped the back of his neck, fingers tangling in his hair, urging him closer. He smirked, his gaze lifting to meet hers as he spread her open with his fingers. Opening his mouth, he pressed his tongue to her inner flesh, causing a bolt like lightning to strike her lower belly. Closing his eyes, he moaned, clamping his lips around her swollen numb. His tongue laved it as he suckled, robbing her of breath. A strangled sound escaped her throat, her heart pounding as the pleasure of the moment and the possibility of being caught caused her blood to surge.

Tightening her grip on his hair, she lifted one leg and draped it over his shoulder, urging him even closer. He tortured her with his tongue, suckling her vulnerable flesh like a starving man, low groans emitting from him to mingle with hers.

One of his fingers found its way inside her, stroking the walls of her pulsating sheath, heightening her pleasure. Bracing her hands on the bench, she raised her hips, urging him deeper. Joining his first finger with his second, he obeyed her silent command for more, quickening his thrusts and delving into her as deep as his third knuckles. His fingers curled inward, finding the secret place inside of her that caused her to bite back a scream.

Goddamn it, he remembered. She, however, had forgotten. It all came back to her now—how well he knew her body, how easy it had been for him to reduce her to a squirming, begging mess in his arms. Once again, she'd underestimated Colin Worthing. A man like him could prove dangerous, as he'd already demonstrated once before.

Closing her eyes, she focused on the sensations he created, anticipating the glorious ending only a few more strokes away. When it finally came, she cried out, unable to hold in her gratification. Trembling, she allowed her hips to fall back to the bench, leaning back as he soothed her with gentle tongue strokes and kisses along the insides of her thighs.

Detecting his movements, she opened her eyes, realizing he now knelt upright between her thighs, tearing at the fastening of his breeches to free the swollen cock pressing against the fabric.

Drawing a sharp breath, she scrambled away from him. She leapt to her feet, lowering her skirts and stepping around him.

Brow furrowed, he braced a hand against the bench and struggled to stand, his injured leg clearly paining him.

"Penny, what are you doing?"

"*Penelope!*" she corrected him, her tone sharp as she reached for her discarded drawers.

Now that she'd achieved completion, she wanted nothing more than to be as far away from him as possible. His nearness became more unnerving by the second.

"I am leaving," she replied with as much dignity as she could while attempting to don her drawers without lifting her skirts too high.

Colin's reddening face and the bulge outlined against his buff-colored breeches gave evidence to his frustration.

"*Penelope*," he growled from between gritted teeth. "We are not finished here."

"I beg to differ," she replied, injecting a great deal of frost into her voice. "I wanted you to pleasure me, and you performed admirably. Now, I am done with you. Honestly, Colin, I am surprised. This is, after all, your *modus operandi*."

One hand clenched into a fist at his side, he took a step toward her. Flinching, she backed away.

"Touch me, and I will scream."

Sighing, he opened his fist and extended his open hand. One of her pearl earrings rested in his palm.

Guilt pricked her conscience, but she forced it down as one would choke down bile. She owed Colin nothing, least of all her sympathy. Snatching the earring from him, she clasped it to her ear, then patted her curls to ensure her coiffure remained presentable.

"I am certain there are many women who would be willing to help you with that," she said, gesturing toward his erection. "As a soldier, I'm certain you're no stranger to whorehouses. But thank you for a most delightful interlude. I do hope you enjoy the rest of our evening."

Turning, she put him behind her, striding toward an opening in the maze.

"I underestimated the effect that my betrayal had on your opinion of me," he murmured.

Despite the softness of his voice, she heard him and turned, wrinkling her brow. "I beg your pardon?"

He remained seated on the bench, his walking stick now grasped in one hand. "Have I hurt you so badly that you think of me as a man who would visit one woman with the taste of another upon my lips? *Your* taste, no less."

Penelope shrugged with a scoff. "I don't know you, Colin. Honestly, I doubt I ever did."

He lowered his gaze and sighed. "I will not argue with you, as you have obviously worked very hard to convince yourself of that. You have a right to your opinion of me, as I have done nothing to prove otherwise. But, I mean to, Penelope. I meant what I said, as well as what you would not allow me to say. I will win you back ... we will marry ... and I will spend the rest of my life changing your opinion of me."

Shaking her head, she began to back away. "Do not bother, Colin. As far as I am concerned, you and I are finished."

Glancing up, he met her gaze with a lopsided grin. "Says the woman who just climaxed in my mouth."

Scowling, she shook her head. "You are an incorrigible cur."

She turned her back to leave once more, but his voice halted her again. Dash it all, why couldn't she simply walk away?

"By the way, I never visited a single whorehouse in Belgium, or anywhere else while abroad. I did not wish to contract some foul disease like many of my fellow soldiers, first and foremost. However, it is not the only reason. The truth is, I have not touched a woman since the night we spent together in that inn ... until now."

Penelope clenched her hands together before her, trying to still their trembling. Her skin tingled, the feel of his eyes on her like a phantom caress. Swallowing past the lump in her throat, she took a deep breath and lifted her chin.

"I don't believe you," she stated, forcing her feet to move, propelling her away from him once and for all.

CHAPTER 4

Colin grunted as he made his way to the lilac drawing room, where he had been told Edmond awaited him. After his disastrous evening, he had returned home and attempted to rest. However, his frazzled nerves, unsatisfied body, and aching leg had made that impossible. He'd spent the entire night tossing and turning in his bed, memories of Penelope's spread legs and wet cunt robbing him of sleep.

Worsening his misery was the pain he'd inflicted on himself in an attempt at seduction. He'd expected the discomfort in his leg caused by kneeling for so long, but had not thought to return home with a cock harder than stone. After several hours of trying to divert his mind elsewhere, he'd given up and allowed his mind to wander to what should have happened in that garden. As he palmed his shaft and stroked, he imagined sitting on that bench with Penelope in his lap, her skirts hitched up around her hips, her tight sheath squeezing him, surrounding him in moisture and heat. His fantasy proved so vivid, he could practically feel her weight on his thighs, taste her sweet nipples in his mouth. It had taken him very little time to climax, his breath rushing out in a deep, guttural sigh of relief.

Yet, relief had been short-lived. Once the euphoria of release had passed, reality had awaited him. He had underestimated the amount of hurt he'd inflicted on Penelope. It became clear that his offense had not been forgotten, nor had it been forgiven. Cursing himself for the fool he'd been, he spent the rest of his evening plotting his next move. Despite her insistence that she cared nothing for him, Colin was not yet ready to concede defeat. His confession to her last night had given her pause. Many things about her had changed, yet he found one thing remained the same. She was not as proficient at hiding her emotions as she pretended to be. Knowing her as well as he did, it was not hard to detect the subtleties marking her emotions—the darting of her eyes, her wavering voice, her posture.

Now that she had exacted her revenge on him, perhaps they could move forward. Thus the reason he had sent a message asking Edmond to visit him during his morning calls. His friend appeared the perfect vision of a gentleman—dove gray morning coat, starched white linen shirt, polished boots, artfully arranged hair. Colin hardly compared at the moment—rumpled shirt and breeches beneath his dressing gown, tousled hair, stubble-ridden jaw. His brothers would be horrified to know he entertained anyone looking this way, even if it was only Edmond. The heir and his spare had always been high in the instep, creating a bit of a chasm between them and their little brother. Colin had always been his own man, and they'd never appreciated that.

"You look like hell," Edmond remarked, amusement tugging at the corners of his mouth. "Did things not go well with Penelope last night?"

He grimaced as he lowered himself into a periwinkle armchair. "That would depend upon one's definition of 'well'."

Edmond chuckled. "So, no, then?"

He shrugged. "I expected tension during our first meeting. Next time will be different."

Arching one eyebrow, Edmond cast him a dubious glance. "Next time? Don't you think you ought to leave the woman alone now,

Colin? You've apologized, she's rung a peal over you ... it is time to move forward."

"I intend to," he announced.

Scowling, Edmond inclined his head. "I don't understand. I thought you said—"

"There will be a next time ... just not for a while," he clarified. "I intend to give Penny her space."

"How very rational of you."

"In the interim, I thought you might help her see that I have changed."

Edmond groaned, burying his face in his hands. "I take it back. You're a madman."

"Just listen, and it will all begin to make sense. You are searching for a wife. From what I have gathered, Penelope has become quite the social butterfly. She knows which ladies come with a fortune, and which come from families saddled with debt. Take her into your confidence and use her knowledge to secure your wealthy bride. Meanwhile, you might allow my name to come up in conversation. You are one of the only people I've spent time with since my return. You can convince her that I am a new man, deserving of another chance."

For a moment, his friend observed him in pensive silence. When he finally spoke again, all traces of humor had fled his tone.

"You really do love her, don't you?"

Colin snorted. "Would I be putting myself through this sort of hell after returning from war if I didn't?"

"Well, the old you might have. Just to prove he could turn her head even after the wrong he'd done."

For the second time, he became forced to confront another person's perception of him, finding it worse than he'd thought. It left a bitter taste in his mouth.

"Am I really such a cad?" he whispered.

"Yes," Edmond replied. "But then, so are many men of the *ton*. We've all had our indiscretions, Colin, and while yours might be more despicable than others, you certainly aren't alone. The difference is, you got caught, while most of our indiscretions remain secret. You're no different than many of our peers."

Lifting his head, he smiled. "So, you'll do it?"

Running a hand through his dark waves, Edmond grunted. "Of course I will. But you must give me adequate time. No haranguing me, and no guarantees it will work."

Colin nodded. "I understand."

"Meanwhile, you might consider lavishing your attentions on some other chit. No woman wants the hat in a milliner's window unless the other ladies are making a fuss over it."

He grimaced. "Must I?"

"Yes," Edmond insisted.

"Drat."

Standing, his friend shrugged, tugging on the lapels of his coat. "The things we do for love ... or in my circumstance, money."

Colin struggled to his feet as well, cursing his leg. "Ed, Penelope is astute. If you make it known you want an amiable match as well as a practical one, she will point you in the right direction."

Edmond turned to him, extending one hand. Colin took it, clasping firm.

"One does not have time for amiable when one is desperate."

As Edmond left and he found himself alone once more, Colin pondered how true that statement proved for him, as well. While he would have liked to go about courting Penelope the right way ... the way he had before ... her current state of mind toward him made that impossible. At this juncture, he felt willing to stoop to any means to win her, even if it meant using his best friend to gain access.

Leaning heavily on his cane, he limped back toward the staircase, determination setting his jaw.

"Better make myself pretty for the ladies," he muttered, scratching a day's worth of beard.

Edmond had been right, after all. If he was going to capture and hold Penelope's attention, he was going to have to pursue someone else while ignoring her completely.

"Bloody games of intrigue," he groused.

For someone who had enjoyed such folly in his youth, Colin found himself longing for an end to it all, preferably with Penelope as his wife, with his child thriving inside her. As far as he was concerned, there could be no other outcome.

Thinking of having her again, of claiming what he'd thrown away with such callousness, had seen him through one of the worst times of his life. While the weeks, months, and years he'd spent away from home had been hard, nothing had compared to Waterloo and its aftermath.

The time before that had stretched on endlessly, a blur of marching across foreign lands, enduring horrid living conditions at times, and even more horrid weather. He'd spent many a night wallowing in his own pitiful misery, mourning what he'd left behind. Letter after letter he had penned to her, only to toss them into the fire, uncertain that she would ever care to read a single word he might write. And how could he explain why he'd done what he had without sounding like the selfish cad he was? Eventually, he had resigned himself to life without her. Still, even when making himself face that reality, he'd refused to take any of the many offers he'd received from whores and camp followers. When he closed his eyes at night, he dreamed of Penelope, of the one beautiful night he'd had with her. He'd truly meant to make her his bride the following day, accepting the gift of her virginity with the intention of being the only man to ever touch her again.

Eventually, he'd found a mechanical sort of contentment in serving at his post, finding that military life suited him. The structure, routine, and discipline had turned a spoiled rake into a responsible soldier—one who had been promoted from second to first lieutenant with a swiftness that surprised many of his peers.

Then, Waterloo had happened, changing everything. The battle that had ended the war had almost claimed his life, as it had taken countless others.

As he'd lay, dying from the poison of infection caused by his leg wound, he'd come to realize his mistake—though clarity had come far too late. The mistake hadn't been that he'd left her, it had been that he'd proposed to her at all. It had been premature, and in his desire to claim her body, he had destroyed any chance at crying off and perhaps postponing such a serious decision until he was well and truly ready. He'd thought himself a man then, but the truth was he'd only been a boy, uncertain and unaware of how his rashness would cost them both.

Perhaps if he'd waited, he might have learned and understand that love could not make a good man of him—that was something he must do on his own. While his actions at Waterloo had been declared heroic, he still had not felt redeemed. He'd known then as he knew now that redemption could only come by setting right what he had destroyed. That meant facing his indiscretion and atoning for it. It meant taking every ounce of abuse Penelope might level at him, for no other reason than he knew he deserved it.

In the end, no lengths were too great, since Colin had realized the truth as he'd hovered on that line between life and death. He could not live without her.

Edmond left Worthing House with a spring in his step and a whistle on his lips. He'd awakened this morning in a chipper mood, and as he neared Hartford House on Brook Street, he realized it had a lot to do with last night's soirée. He hadn't enjoyed an evening more in a long while. Considering his earlier dread over this Season, it seemed quite an accomplishment. Even though he'd ribbed Colin for involving him in his conquest to win Penelope, he enjoyed the notion of acting as proxy between them. It reminded him of the days of his youth, when the Season had been some new and exciting thing, a time to flirt with the fresh, young debutantes. Given all that rested upon his shoulders with his family troubles and the bankrupt estate he would inherent, this would provide a pleasant distraction.

Besides, he'd enjoyed his conversation with Penelope last night during the quadrille. She'd been witty, funny, and charming. Few women existed like her among those of the *ton*. It was no wonder Colin was determined to have her.

Arriving at 39, Brook Street, home of the Marquis of Hartford and his family, he took the steps to the front door two at a time before knocking. A properly staunch butler answered, accepting his card. After announcing he had come to call on the marchioness, he was ushered into a sitting room decorated entirely in pink. Floral damask furniture overwhelmed the room, its rosy curtains a perfect match for the blossoms in crystal vases upon every available surface.

The marchioness had obviously dressed to heighten the effect, a mauve morning gown trimmed in white lace causing her to appear as a blossom in a garden. She rose, curtsying as he approached, bowing in return. She then allowed him to take her hand and brush a chaste kiss against the knuckles.

"Lady Hartford," he murmured, giving her his most charming smile. "How good it is to see you again. You're looking quite lovely this morning, I must say. That particular shade of pink compliments your coloring to perfection."

Smiling, she motioned for him to sit, lowering herself gracefully on the loveseat. "Lord Ingham, you are, and always have been, a shameless flatterer."

He sat in a high-backed chair upholstered in red and pink roses, hands braced on his thighs. "Only when in the company of beautiful women."

"Will you take tea with me, my lord?" she offered, gesturing toward the tea service and an array of cakes laid out in a three-tiered silver platter before them.

Impatience niggled at him, but the proper courtesies must be observed first. "Of course, my lady. I would be delighted."

They conducted mundane chatter as she poured his tea, quickly answering his question concerning her health that she was 'quite well' before inquiring whether he wished for lemon, sugar, or milk. She served it in porcelain china, placing a biscuit on the saucer beside his cup. She inquired after his health, and that of his father while preparing her own tea, then remarked on the fair weather.

Edmond finished half his tea and biscuit before arriving at his reason for visiting. "I had wondered, Lady Hartford, if Lady Penelope is at home. I had hoped to invite her to take a walk with me."

Setting her saucer aside, the lady stood and rang for a servant. "I can certainly inquire, my lord."

The butler appeared at the door, and after a swift exchange, disappeared once more. Edmond polished off his tea and biscuit, and thanked his hostess. He fought to keep from bouncing his leg and tapping his fingers against the arm of his chair.

It seemed like an eternity before Penelope appeared, wearing a walking dress in white muslin trimmed in spring green with a matching spencer, a straw bonnet clutched between her slender fingers, its green ribbon dangling. He stood when he spied her, clearing his throat of the sudden vise that gripped it. She was radiant, the springtime hues of her ensemble causing the red tones of her hair to appear far brighter, catching the light of the sun streaming through the windows.

"Lady Penelope," he said, inclining his head. "One would have to be blind not to notice that you've inherited your mother's beauty. You look positively divine. I hope you are well this morning."

The smile she gave him was sunny, genuine. He'd seen her afflict a far more affected smile on the men at the ball last evening—something she'd likely practiced and perfected over the years. He found himself relieved at the sight of her true smile.

"Thank you, my lord. I am quite well. And you?"

He extended an arm to her. "Better now," he murmured under his breath.

Edmond had no notion of what caused him to wish to flirt with her. It was uncouth, really, when Colin had sent him to her on a specific mission. However, just as it had during their quadrille, the urge had been hard to ignore, the words coming to his mouth before he could stop them. It did not help that she seemed to find it amusing, and had answered in kind.

Her lips curved into a smirk as she placed her hand in the crook of his arm. "Shall we?"

"By all means," he replied, leading her toward the door. "Have a pleasant afternoon, Lady Hartford."

Penelope mumbled good-bye to her mother, then they walked out into the sunny afternoon and down the front steps.

"Well, this is a pleasant surprise, my lord," she remarked as they began strolling at a leisurely pace.

He darted a glance at her from the corner of his eye. "Oh, but you must have known I would call today ... after last evening."

She grinned at him. "Ah, so you *did* enjoy our quadrille as much as I did. I was not entirely certain."

"A man would have to be daft not to enjoy your company in any situation, Lady Penelope."

"Just Penelope, please," she insisted. "With the majority of the *ton* in Hyde Park this time of day, there is no one around to hear you address me thus, and I insist. Or Penny, if you like."

First names already ... this would be easier than he had first surmised.

"Then you must call me Edmond, or Ed. And, I did enjoy our dance, but I admit to seeking to satisfy my own curiosity. How did you get on with Colin last night?"

Her hold tightened on his arm, and he noted the downward curve of her mouth.

"I'd rather not discuss him, if you don't mind."

Damnation. What had the idiot said to upset her?

"Of course, I apologize. I merely asked out of concern for you. I know it could not have been easy, confronting him after all this time."

Her brow creased and she halted in her tracks, forcing him to pause as her hand closed around his elbow. He found himself yanked off-balance when she whirled suddenly, pulling him into the alley between two townhouses. Turning on him once they were out of sight, she folded her arms across her chest.

"What do you know about it?"

Edmond grimaced, unable to believe he'd made such a gaffe. As far as the rest of the *ton* was concerned, the only thing that had occurred between Penelope and Colin was a Season of courting, which had ended—shockingly—in no betrothal. While there had been speculation as to the reason, nothing with the power to smudge her reputation had been discovered, thus the gossip had died a swift death.

Against his better judgement, he reached out and touched her, gripping her shoulders with gentle hands.

"Everything," he admitted. "Upon leaving you in Gretna Green, Colin came to me first. He was shaking, sweating ... out of his mind with fear and guilt over what he had done. I urged him to go back for you and do the right thing."

She snorted. "The two of you must not be very good friends if he did not listen."

He laughed. "You know how tenacious he can be. Colin insisted you would have woken to find him missing already, and that he'd left a note. His chance with you was ruined and there was no going back. That was when I told him he needed to leave."

Penelope gasped, a hand coming up over her mouth. "I always assumed his father had been responsible."

"Lord Worthing saw to the specifics and purchased the commission at Colin's behest, but I was the one who told him to go. I reminded him to think of you and not himself. How awful it would have been for you to be forced to socialize with him Season after Season, knowing what had occurred at that inn. The hope was that you'd be wed with a child or two by the time he returned."

She snorted, her eyes darting upward as if she searched the heavens for what remained of his good sense. "Typical. I can assure you, I do not need a husband to aid me in moving past what happened. I have moved forward with my life on my own, and intend to continue to do so ... alone."

Despite the strength of her tone, he could see the uncertainty in her gaze. Edmond saw the truth as clearly as if she'd spoken it aloud.

Tightening his hold on her shoulders, he gave her a gentle nudge, urging her closer. She tilted her head back, meeting his gaze without hesitation. He saw a great deal in the depths of her stare—a bit of sadness, a hard glint that indicated just how jaded she'd become, and something else he dared not accept. Yet, how could he ignore the way her lips parted as her gaze became downright sensual? Quite an unexpected occurrence, that.

Could Penelope feel attraction toward *him*? He'd thought her simply flirting for the sake of fun, yet he knew well what that gaze meant.

He cleared his throat and shook his head, fighting the urge to respond the way he typically did when a woman stared at him that way.

"Won't you ever marry?" he murmured.

She shook her head. "Why? I am quite firmly on the shelf and set to receive my inheritance soon."

"Because," he whispered. "Look at you. For a woman like you to live her life without passion—without love—is the saddest thing I could ever imagine."

Smirking, she gripped the lapels of his coat and leaned into him. Her curves pressed against his hard planes, causing an inevitable reaction. His gut clenched, his blood heating in his veins and rushing straight to his groin.

"I never said I intended to live without passion," she whispered. "Being alone does not mean I must be lonely. I enjoy the company of a man whenever I please. It is most satisfying."

Edmond's throat constricted and his cock pulsed in his breeches, seeming to respond to her words. What was this? Penelope and Colin shared unfinished business, and despite her insistence that she had moved past it, Edmond knew better. Besides, he was supposed to be here for Colin, not himself.

Yet, nothing could have stopped him from moving his hands, skimming them down her shoulders and back, then lower to the swell of her buttocks. She gasped when he drew her toward him, pressing the evidence of his arousal against her belly. Satisfaction pulled his mouth into a smirk at her reaction, a startled gasp, then a low moan as he shifted his hips, letting her feel just what she had done to him.

Whimpering, she came up on tiptoe and claimed his mouth, smoothing the palms of her hands up over his chest. With an answering groan, he grasped her hips and lifted her, propelling her back against the brick façade of the house behind them. His hat fell from his head, tumbling among the refuse littering the alley, and her fingers traveled up into his hair, caressing his scalp as their mouths moved together in a synchronized dance.

She claimed him boldly, kissing with more skill than an inexperienced woman of her age ought. But then, she was not inexperienced, and if her words proved true, she'd taken other lovers since Colin. The notion sent another surge of fire through his veins, as he realized he could be next. She wanted him; he wanted her ... there was nothing stopping him from taking what she so blatantly offered.

Except Colin.

Edmond tore his mouth from hers, fighting to catch his breath and clear his senses. As it was, he'd become overwhelmed by Penelope— her scent, the feel of her body his arms, the sight of her kiss-swollen mouth and lowered eyelids.

"Penny, I cannot."

Her eyes flew open, widening. "Why not? It is clear that we feel attraction toward each other. I've enjoyed your company—both last night, and this morning. Can you say you have not enjoyed mine?"

Sighing, he ran a hand through his mussed hair, turning to search for his hat. "Of course I have. But, you know why. Colin—"

"Is a cad," she interjected.

"Is a changed man," he corrected. "Have you any notion what going to war does to a man? It forces him to face death, which allows him to understand how life ought to be lived. Despite his failings, he does love you, and I do not think he will ever stop. I am his best friend, so this cannot be about what I want."

"I have told you, Colin is no longer a part of my life. I do not love him, and I have no intention of allowing him to manipulate and lie to me again."

Dusting off his hat, he placed it back on his head, extending his arm to her once more. "I understand, and I believe you. But I cannot in good conscience take what you offer … no matter how badly I might wish to."

Sighing, she accepted his arm and allowed him to lead her from the alley. He reversed their direction, deciding he needed to remove himself from her presence posthaste. Another moment alone with her in that alley and he wouldn't have been able to stop himself from lifting her skirts and fucking her until she screamed.

Gritting his teeth, he kept his gaze straight ahead and tried to clear his mind of the images that thought conjured.

When her family's home came into view once more, she spoke.

"I apologize for my advance," she murmured. "I misunderstood your intentions, and it will not happen again."

Devil take it, this had not happened the way he'd planned. What was worse, he'd caused her to feel guilt, which might make her avoid him—the opposite of what he needed. His pitiful attempt at convincing her to give Colin another chance hadn't been enough. He needed to try again.

"Please, do not apologize. It is my fault. You're a beautiful woman, and for a moment, I forgot what you mean to someone I care a great deal about. This is not about you, Penelope. If it weren't for him—"

"Many things might be different," she muttered, her tone holding the edge of bitterness.

Pausing before the front steps, he turned to face her. "You aren't angry with me, are you?"

Smiling up at him, she bit her lower lip—a motion that did not help the situation causing his breeches to remain painfully snug.

"Edmond, I doubt anyone could remain angry with you for long."

"Then I may count you among my friends?"

"Of course."

"Good. A party of friends and I have plans to ride to Richmond Park Friday afternoon. We thought an escape from the city might be in order. We're to make a day of it, share a picnic, that sort of thing."

She pursed her lips. "I take it Colin will be among your 'friends'?"

He shrugged. "Yes, but you won't let that spoil the day, will you? You shall be my guest, and will not be forced to speak to him beyond the obligatory greetings if you wish. Besides, I am certain you've heard I am seeking a wife this Season. A few of my prospects will be there, though I confess to not knowing much about them. As a seasoned woman of the *ton*, I thought you might possess the knowledge to guide me in the right direction."

While she seemed to think on it for a moment, her gaze wandered beyond him, her mouth twisting in an adorable habit he doubted she noticed.

"It sounds like a wonderful afternoon," she replied. "And since we have decided that we are friends, I am happy to guide you in your pursuit of a bride."

He grinned, relieved that he had not ruined an opportunity to bring Colin and Penelope together, as well as taking advantage of her knowledge about the other women of the *ton*.

"Brilliant," he said. "Shall I come for you at noon? We can make the drive together. I'd enjoy the opportunity to spend more time with you … my new friend."

She laughed, nodding as she turned to ascend the steps. "Noon, it is. Thank you, Edmond, for an … interesting experience."

He smiled at her, lifting a hand to wave goodbye when she glanced down at him over her shoulder. Her answering grin caused him to feel something different than the lust that had crippled him earlier. As if a vise had gripped his chest, giving it a powerful squeeze at the sight of her smile.

"Dear God, I am losing my mind," he muttered as he began making his way home to dress for dinner and the evening ahead.

He held out hope that, between now and Friday, he might forget the feel of her in his arms.

CHAPTER 5

*P*enelope forced a smile and attempted to focus on the conversation taking place between her and three other ladies. She had been invited to attend a rather large dinner party by her friend, Lady Cecily Cranfield. Cecily and her husband had turned the gathering into a yearly affair, in what Penelope saw as a blatant attempt at matchmaking. Every invited guest, with the exception of the host and hostess, were eligible bachelors and debutantes. While Cecily knew Penelope was determined to avoid marriage, she invited her anyway, still holding out hope that love would change her mind. Apparently, being deliriously happy with her own husband meant her friend would not rest until every eligible female she knew experienced the same.

She'd hope the evening would prove a pleasant distraction from the events of the afternoon and last evening's ball. Her dreams last night had been filled with memories of Colin hunched between her thighs, his tongue stroking her to completion. Intermingled with those recollections were thoughts of the night they'd spent together at the guesthouse in Gretna Green. For all his faults, Colin's skill as a lover could not be denied. While she had taken other amours since him, no other had come close to satisfying her the way he had. She'd awakened from her erotic dreams in a cold sweat, the pulsations between her thighs unbearable.

And now, Edmond Ingham had gone and kissed her, furthering her curiosity about him. If anyone possessed the potential to satisfy her sexual needs, it would be him. His kiss had been filled with promise, his hands strong, long-fingered, and downright beautiful. She'd wanted those hands on her so badly, he'd nearly reduced her to begging. Yet, he'd insisted on playing the gentleman, which had only made her want him more.

Blast both men for leaving her so out of sorts! This kind of thing was the reason she avoided the marriage trap. She had grown used to being in control—selecting her lovers, and dictating the terms of their arrangement. Now, she found herself lusting after two men; one who did not deserve it, and another who did, yet had refused.

To add insult to injury, Colin had been invited to Cecily's little soirée, thus the reason for her distraction. Despite being in good company, which included her best friend, Penelope found herself unable to contribute to the conversation. It became difficult to focus when Colin looked so dashing in his black evening clothes and white linen. The fit of his black breeches displayed powerful thighs, while the tailoring of his coat exhibited powerful shoulders. His starched, white cravat reached up toward his ears, accenting the strong line of his jaw.

Licking his lips, he took a sip of amber liquid from his tumbler, causing her to remember the busy muscle wreaking havoc on her wet cunt. Swallowing past the lump in her throat, she clenched her thighs together to squelch the yearning there.

She didn't want him ... she did *not*.

"Penny," Cecily hissed, gaining her attention.

She blinked, tearing her gaze from Colin to find that dinner had been announced, and the guests had begun lining up in order of rank. As hostess, Cecily should have been at the front of the line, yet had been sidetracked by her woolgathering friend.

Smiling sheepishly, she stood, smoothing her skirts. "I'm sorry. My mind must have wandered."

Cecily nodded, but gave her an assessing glance. "I shouldn't have invited him, should I? I'm so sorry, Penny, I did not think."

Realizing she referred to Colin, Penelope forced a smile. "Oh, no, don't be silly. I have hardly given it a second thought."

"Yes, but, according to rank … well …"

"What she is trying to tell you is that I am your escort and dinner companion," Colin said, appearing at her side.

Her throat was seized as if by a closed fist, his nearness disarming her. His overwhelmingly masculine scent permeated the air around them, causing her mouth to water.

Clearing her throat, she forced herself to meet his gaze with a shrug. "I knew that. Why should I become bothered by it?"

Cecily appeared dubious, but had no choice but to leave her in Colin's company to take her place at the front of the line. As they waited for their turn to leave the drawing room, she and Colin stood side by side and waited for the guests who outranked them to file out first.

"You look well, my lady," he remarked, offering her his arm.

She took it, surprised at his formal addressing of her. Keeping her gaze fixed straight ahead, she avoided his stare.

"Save your flatteries for the woman seated on your other side," she whispered. "I am not speaking to you."

From the corner of her eye, she saw him nod.

"Very well."

They lapsed into silence, though she remained all-too aware of his nearness. As they filed into the dining room, she felt relief that he obeyed her request and did not attempt to engage her in small talk like the other pairs in the room. He pulled her chair out for her, then seated himself. As the first course was served, he promptly turned his attention to the lady seated to his left—Sybil Beauchamp, daughter of Baron Beauchamp.

A lovely young woman with coils of golden blonde hair and large, blue eyes, she seemed all-too happy to oblige Colin by engaging him in conversation. Her smile grew wide, her eyes large with wonder as she fell under the spell of his smooth charm. Gripping her spoon tight, Penelope turned her attention to the white soup before her, though her ears were attuned to the conversation occurring just to her right.

"I cannot imagine what it must be like, Captain," the young chit murmured, "to go to war. You must have been so brave."

"A brave man can still be a frightened one," he replied. "However, one does his duty despite that fear. Now that the war is won, I find myself fortunate to have returned home. The food is far superior … as is the company."

Penelope gritted her teeth as Sybil simpered, lowering her head demurely to avoid his gaze. They continued this way through the soup course, only pausing as the main dish was served. She engaged in forced small talk with Colin as he followed the ritual of offering her the dishes nearest him as his duty as her dinner companion dictated. The moment their plates had been filled, he turned back to Sybil, taking a marked interest in her description of a watercolor painting she'd begun that morning.

By the time the dessert course arrived, Penelope had grown overcome with the urge to take up her knife and drive it through her ear. The sound of Sybil's laughter—simpering and shrill—along with Colin's smooth baritone voice set her on edge.

As the night wore on, it became increasingly difficult to pretend she did not recognize the feeling in the pit of her stomach for what it truly was.

Jealousy.

Colin's valet had just finished shaving him when a footman appeared at the door of his chambers to announce a visitor. Frowning, he fished his watch from the pocket of his waistcoat. He was due at Sybil Beauchamp's residence in fifteen minutes, and they had the long drive to Richmond Park ahead of them. It would be the longest amount of time he'd spent in the company of such an intimate group since his return, and it had taken him much mental preparation to grow used to the idea. He was still unaccustomed to being peppered with questions concerning Belgium, Waterloo, or the injury to his leg —all things that became inevitable the more intimate the social situation.

Grimacing, he snapped the watch closed and asked the footman to escort the visitor to a drawing room. A caller before the socially acceptable hours could only mean one thing. This was business, and he doubted it was the military sort. Colin had a vague idea of who awaited him as he retrieved his walking stick and descended the staircase.

Sure enough, when he entered the parlor, he found William Claremont, Marquis of Hartford, awaiting him. Penelope's stepfather. Because of his father's swift actions in securing a commission for him, Colin had never faced the man who possessed the power to force him to marry Penelope after ruining her.

It would seem time had done little to lessen the man's dislike of him. If anything, the deepening lines of age creasing his weathered face only enhanced the clear disdain on the man's face.

Not that Colin could blame him.

"My lord," he murmured, closing the doors behind him so they could not be heard. "I would say it is a pleasure, but considering the early hour, I assume you are not here to exchange pleasantries. Shall we come right to the matter at hand? You are here concerning Penelope."

The marquis folded his arms across his barrel-wide chest and stared down his nose at Colin. Despite his advanced age, the man was as massive as an oak, and in prime physical condition. Colin didn't doubt he could deliver quite a bout of fisticuffs if necessary.

"Captain," he replied curtly. "You're correct, this is not a social call. I heard you were Penelope's dinner companion at Lord and Lady Cranfield's dinner party last evening. I also have it on authority that you will be attending a picnic in Richmond Park today in a group of acquaintances that will also include her."

He inclined his head. "My lord seems awfully interested in my social calendar."

Hartford took a menacing step toward him, and Colin could have sworn he heard the floorboards groan beneath the rug.

"Keep your impertinent tongue behind your teeth unless it is to answer my questions. Now ... are you purposely pursuing Penelope with any intent at all, salacious or not?"

Why yes, my lord. Despite the fact that I ruined her and left her high and dry three years ago, I am in love with her and determined to make her my wife.

Those words would likely not be well received, despite them being the truth. Colin decided to attempt a modified form of the truth.

"No," he replied. "I approached her at the Duke and Duchess of Avonleah's ball, hoping to apologize for my action and begin anew. She spurned me, making it clear she has no desire to renew our acquaintance. Last night's dinner party and today's picnic are mere coincidences placing us in the same company—a circumstance that is to be expected as long as we are both unwed and share friends of the same age."

Hartford seemed to consider this for a moment, observing him with a dubious eye. "See to it that you respect Penelope's wishes. It is bad enough she must tolerate your presence now that the infernal war is over. I'll not countenance you hurting her again."

"Hurting Penelope is the last thing I wish to do. Returning was something I could not avoid, and now that I am here, I wish to move forward with my life. Now, if you will excuse me, my lord, a young lady is awaiting me ... we do not wish to be late arriving at Richmond."

Taking another step toward him, Hartford towered over him until they stood nearly nose-to-nose. "I'm watching you, Captain. See to it that you treat any young lady in your company with the respect you failed to show my daughter, or I will ensure you suffer an unfortunate accident."

Colin bit back a scathing retort. It lay on the tip of his tongue to tell this chap to sod off, and that he had not faced death at the hand of Boney's soldiers to feel fear in the face of a stodgy old man. However, he knew it would gain him nothing to anger the man who had raised Penelope. Once he had won her heart again, he was going to need the marquis' permission to marry her—hopefully with much coercion from her.

"You are justified in your concerns, my lord, but I can assure you my time in Belgium has changed me profoundly. I am not the same person I was when I left. My behavior going forward will be beyond reproach."

The marquis glanced down at his walking stick and injured leg, his expression softening. News of his injury had spread upon his return, though the circumstances around it remained his own secret.

Giving him an abrupt nod, the marquis marched toward the doors to the parlor. "See that it is."

Once the doors closed behind his future father-in-law, Colin lowered his head and released a sigh of relief. That could have ended far worse than it had, and he felt proud of himself for keeping his temper at bay.

He waited until the front door opened and closed before he left the room, encountering the butler, who stood by with his hat and coat.

"Thank you, Ruthers," he murmured before exiting the house and bounding down the steps toward his waiting phaeton.

Climbing up onto the perch, he steeled himself for an afternoon of torture. He couldn't think of anything worse than feigning interest in a woman with the personality of a lamppost while secretly hoping to make the woman he loved jealous.

CHAPTER 6

The day of the outing to Richmond Park brought pleasant weather. Seated on the perch of his gig with Penelope at his side, Edmond lightly held the reins. The road before them lay vacant, with the picturesque scenery of the countryside framing it. London had become an afterthought, left behind over half an hour ago. They made good time, and he estimated they would arrive to Richmond Park first, unless one of the other pairs had left earlier than they had.

Penelope shone radiant in a carriage dress of pale yellow muslin, a white spencer trimmed in lace buttoned just beneath her breasts. A white hat pinned with matching flowers covered her head, and a few locks of her auburn hair caressed the side of her neck, continually drawing his stare.

Clenching his jaw, he forced his gaze back to the road, reminding himself that he must be on his best behavior today. Never mind the fact that he hadn't been able to chase memories of Penelope's kiss from his mind, or that the desire to repeat the experience never seemed far off. He'd invited Penelope on this outing for the sole purpose of forcing her into close proximity with Colin—*not* to spend more time with her himself.

Clearing his throat, he fumbled for a subject of conversation. "Have you ever been to Richmond Park?"

Turning to stare at him, she gave a wistful smile. "I haven't been since I was a child. Before my father died, he would surprise Mother and me with picnic baskets on sunny afternoons. We would drive to the park and spend hours there."

Edmond snuck another glance at her. "How old were you when he died?"

"Five," she replied.

"I'm so sorry," he murmured. "I cannot imagine."

His financial woes suddenly seemed minute compared to life without one's parent.

Smiling at him, she shrugged. "I miss him, but the pain of it has faded. It's more an occasional longing. I suppose that is because I've had Hartford since the age of seven. He could not sire children of his own, so he took me as his daughter. He has treated me with more love and affection than I could have imagined a person might feel for a child not their own."

That the marquis doted on Penelope as his own daughter did not bode well for Colin. The man would not stand for him attempting to worm his way back into her good graces after having ruined and abandoned her.

"I am glad for you," he replied. "My father is quite a bit more ... complicated."

Brow wrinkled, she gave him a curious glance. "I'm sorry?"

Sighing, he pursed his lips. He did not know what possessed him to want to tell her his shameful secret. He told himself it must be her eyes—so wide and guileless, genuine with curiosity and concern. They made him feel like telling her everything he'd ever thought or felt, no matter how shameful. The back of his neck grew hot, and his tongue became thick and unwieldy, useless inside his mouth.

Smiling at him, she placed her hand on his knee. The touch seared him to the bone, causing the muscle to grow tense at her fingertips.

"It's all right," she murmured, seeming oblivious to the effect he had on him. "You don't have to speak of it if you don't want. But ... we *did* decide we are friends. Nothing you could tell me would cause me to think poorly of you. I admire you very much, Edmond."

Christ, what was it about this woman that made him feel so exposed? He wanted to be held by her. He wanted to say to her all the things that he dared not. He wanted what he had no right to.

He forced a smile. "Ah, I'm certain you've heard the story before. Only son of a nobleman is born to a family with high expectations. Rigorous education, opulent lifestyle ... one that the young man learns is all a farce protecting a dark family secret. Suffice it to say, if I don't nab a wealthy wife this Season, I might see all our possessions sold at auction and find us all shamed due to lack of credit."

She gasped, her expression morphing into one of horror and pity. "Oh, Edmond, how awful."

He shrugged. "I can no longer avoid the marriage trap. So ... your help in scouting out potential mates is most welcome. I would like to marry someone amiable, as well as wealthy. She doesn't need to be highly intelligent, but I'd like to be able to hold a conversation with her. I want to *like* her, at least. I have no delusions about love."

With a frown, she edged closer to him on the gig's perch, her hand still lying on his thigh. His throat constricted, and he found himself wishing she'd trail those slender digits of hers a bit higher.

"That sounds ever so boring," she whispered, her eyes glittering with mischief.

Unable to resist, he quirked one brow and smirked. "Does it?"

"Mm-hmm," she murmured. "That is why I do not believe in marriage. Very few *ton* unions are based on anything more than business—what one may offer the other to advance their position."

"What about your mother? She seems happy with Hartford."

"An exception to the rule. Marriage is a farce; one I have no desire to participate in. I prefer a life of freedom ... of passion. I'd rather live in the moment with someone, with no thought of tomorrows, than be trapped in monotony, facing the same stale courtesies and predicable routine day after day."

She sat so close now he could smell her—an enticing scent that seemed uniquely hers. His will had fled, and as they arrived at Richmond Park, he pulled the gig to a halt and gave her his full attention. They sat alone, as none of their companions had arrived yet. The serenity and solitude of the picturesque park emboldened him, and he indulged himself by leaning closer, lowering his face toward the curve of her neck. Her hat shaded them, stray strands of her hair tickling his nose and lips. Her scent grew stronger, tickling his nostrils and seeming to invade every crevice of his head until felt as if he drowned in her. Awareness sent a tingle down the back of his neck, which traveled the length of his spine and coiled in his groin, spreading outward in a warm rush.

"That sounds like a wonderful fantasy," he whispered, nuzzling her neck. "I only wish I were fortunate enough to partake in such a relationship."

She lowered her head, skimming her lips along the line of his jaw. Their mouths hovered inches apart, their breaths mingling in the quiet of the afternoon. He gripped her chin with his fingers, moving her until their lips brushed—not connecting, but caressing in short, languid strokes. Hers parted, and he detected the quickening of her breath.

"You could," she whispered. "At least, until the Season ends and you make an offer to your bride. One last indulgence."

His thumb stroked her chin, then her lower lip. Whimpering, she brought her tongue forward, flicking it out to caress the pad of his finger. He groaned, sliding his hand back to grasp her neck.

"I would … if there were only a woman I wanted badly enough to entice into such an arrangement."

She shivered in his hold, tilting her head back as if inviting his kiss. His gut clenched, his entire being aching as hunger echoed through him. He'd just made up his mind to take her mouth with his, when the thud of horses' hooves and clatter of carriage wheels alerted him that someone approached.

"Goddamn it," he muttered, pulling away with a sharp gasp.

Her eyelids fluttered several times as she blinked, seeming to clear her head. Sitting up straight, she moved away from him on the perch before the other conveyance came into view, her hand snatching away from his thigh as if it had just grown unbearably hot.

Cheeks flushed, she lowered her gaze, refusing to meet his stare, hands folded in her lap. Had she just offered him the passion she'd spoken of? With her?

Edmond grew aroused at the thought of Penelope naked and spread beneath him, legs around his waist, breasts bouncing and nipples tickling his chest as he thrust between her hips, his cock buried deep in her honeyed sheath. He wanted it, more than he'd been willing to admit after their first kiss. Yet again, he reminded himself that she was not his to want. To pursue her when Colin loved her would be the height of betrayal, and against the unspoken gentleman's code. He was not that sort of man.

"I'm sorry, Penny," he whispered before alighting from the gig. "I can't."

Penelope nibbled on cucumber sandwiches, her gaze lowered to the blanket she shared with Edmond. On the warm grass around them, four other pairs shared blankets, as well as hampers of food. Chatter exchanged between them, as well as delicacies brought from home. She had tasted lemon tartlets from Miss Miranda York's kitchen, blackberry jam and cakes from Rose Weatherby's cook, and sumptuous cream puffs provided by Sybil Beauchamp.

The supplier of said cream puffs sat beside Colin on the blanket across from her and Edmond, looking as pretty as a portrait in white muslin, her hat removed and pale blonde ringlets framing her face. Her doll-like features caused her to appear porcelain, yet she was anything but cold. Soft smiles and tinkling laughter drew the attention of all their companions ... Colin, most of all.

His attention was rapt upon Sybil, his eyes twinkling as he murmured to her in hushed tones, his smile wide, his laughter deep and throaty. Every time he chuckled, the sound stroked her spine like a caress, flooding her veins with warmth. The light of the sun caused his hair to gleam like a halo ... yet this man was no angel. As he plucked a grape from the bunch he shared with Sybil, she watched him bring it to his mouth. Her lips parted of their own volition when he parted his. His gaze lifted to meet hers as his tongue caressed the round fruit before he enveloped it, biting down. He licked his lips, causing heat to pool in her belly, spreading down between her thighs. Memories of his tongue tickling her clit made her grow moist as a low pulsation began within her core.

A strong hand found hers, and she started, turning to find Edmond gazing at her in concern. She realized that he was waiting for her to speak—likely having asked a question she had not heard, having been too busy staring at Colin.

Pull yourself together, she chastised herself. *It is Edmond you want! Besides, Colin has perfect little Sybil to keep him company. He has moved on, and so should you.*

She gave Edmond a sheepish smile as she realized he'd spoken and she hadn't heard a word. "I'm sorry ... my mind wandered for a moment. What did you say?"

"Would you like to walk a bit? It seems everyone has finished eating. I don't know about you, but I'd like to stretch my legs and take in more of the scenery."

Glancing around, she found that the others had begun packing the remains of their picnics into their baskets and folding their blankets. Taking Edmond's offered hand, she rose.

"That sounds wonderful," she replied, keeping her attention on him and trying to ignore Colin.

As it was, being in the company of both men had her on edge, causing butterflies to beat their wings inside their belly, and her palms to grow moist. The moment she'd shared with Edmond in the gig remained foremost in her mind, while memories from the night of the Avonleah ball with Colin assailed her as well. Having them both on either side of her, their presences overwhelming and masculine, made a muddle of her thoughts and a ruin of her senses. A walk seemed just the thing to take the edge off.

She took Edmond's arm, and they set off down a winding path behind the other couples. A gently moving stream flanked them on their left, with a great expanse of trees and foliage to their right. Birds chirped among the boughs, and the sun glinted off the surface of the water. A more romantic setting could not be asked for. Too bad she was forced to suffer Colin's presence and the tittering Sybil Beauchamp, who gasped in delight over a flitting butterfly, prompting Colin to point out a mallard duck drifting on the river—which only provoked more girlish squeals and an infuriatingly endearing clap of her hands.

Penelope found herself stomping over the ground with fists clenched, her teeth grinding together. She did not want to feel the sickening sensation swirling in her belly, nor did she wish to acknowledge the reason for it. What she wanted was to put as much distance between herself and Colin as possible. As well, a bit of space from Edmond might do her some good.

"Go on without me," she murmured, halting and dislodging her arm from Edmond's. "I've grown a bit tired. I think I'll return to the blankets and rest until you all return."

The entire group halted, having heard her.

"Surely, you cannot return alone," Sybil said, clinging to one of Colin's arms with both hands. "Captain, perhaps we should return with her. You could rest your leg."

Colin gave her a strained smile. "My leg is fine, Miss Beauchamp, but if Lady Penelope requires an escort, we could go back with her."

"Oh, no," Penelope insisted. "I'll be all right on my own. I do not want to keep you all from your walk."

"I've had quite enough of walking," chimed in Miss Weatherby. "I'll be more than happy to accompany you, Miss Hunt."

The amiable company of Rose Weatherby was preferable to that of the two men whose presence threatened her sanity.

"Thank you, Miss Weatherby," she said, falling in step with her new companion.

"I shall come, too," Sybil decided, dislodging from Colin. "We will see the gentleman after your walk. Enjoy!"

With a sunny smile, she reached for Penelope, linking arms with her as if they were lifelong friends.

Forced to continue on the path back to their picnic spot, Penelope fought the overwhelming urge to scratch the other woman's eyes out.

CHAPTER 7

Colin kept his gaze on the uneven terrain passing beneath his feet, gingerly placing one foot in front of the other. While he grew stronger by the day, he still felt uncertain that his leg would hold up if he planted his foot in a hole, or stubbed it on a large rock. Grimacing, he leaned more heavily on his cane, fighting to keep his breath level and his expression neutral. The last thing he needed from his companions was pity.

Nonetheless, he could feel Edmond's gaze on his back, and knew his friend had chosen to take up the rear in order to keep his eye on him. Pausing, he allowed their group to continue on without them, realizing that he and Edmond had fallen behind.

Panting, he removed his handkerchief from his coat pocket and dabbed at his glistening forehead.

"You're exhausted," Edmond observed, coming up beside him. "Perhaps you should have remained behind with Sybil and Penelope."

Replacing the linen within his breast pocket, Colin snorted. "No, thank you. If I had to continue on in that farce with Miss Beauchamp for another moment, I might have screamed."

"Ah," he replied. "I see. Well, the others may continue on for a while yet before they start back in this direction. Shall we try to catch them up, or lie in wait for them to return and join the group, pretending we never left it?"

He grinned. "The second suggestion sounds vastly more appealing. Where shall we hide to lie in wait?"

"There." Edmond pointed to the line of trees flanking them. "See the fallen log? You can sit there and rest your leg. Come."

Scowling, he narrowed his eyes at his friend's offered arm. "I can manage it."

Shrugging one shoulder, Edmond retained his stoic expression. "Humor me, Colin."

He accepted the assistance, grateful for it even as he complained under his breath that Edmond treated him like an old woman. With searing pains shooting down from hip to thigh like lightning strikes, he certainly felt like one at the moment. He sighed with relief once they reached the fallen log Edmond had indicated. The trees hid them from the path, offering them a small measure of privacy. Laying his walking stick at his feet, he braced his hands against the rough bark.

"Peace, at last."

Edmond chuckled. "Miss Beauchamp is a lovely woman."

"That is true enough. She's a beauty. Just a bit … vapid for my taste."

"Penelope is seething with envy," Edmond murmured. "I've been watching her since you and Miss Beauchamp arrived, and it could not be more plain. She might have tried to convince me she cares nothing for you, but her actions do not lie. The attention you are lavishing on Sybil … it's working."

Nodding, he ran a hand through his hair. "Good. Then I'll do what I can to ensure we are together in Penelope's presence as much as possible. Though that will prove harder than I'd anticipated. Hartford called on me at home this morning. He is on to me, I think. The man warned me quite bluntly to keep my distance. He is following my every move."

"Hmm," Edmond hummed. "That could present a problem. Unless

… I become Penelope's escort. If I am with her, we can coordinate our appearances to coincide with yours, ensuring your aims are achieved with neither Penelope nor Hartford the wiser. Besides, the more attention you pay to Miss Beauchamp in public, the less likely the marquis is to suspect what you are up to. Until you secure Penelope's promise to marry, of course."

Colin shrugged. "He will bluster at first, but he loves Penny. If he hears her say with her own lips that she has accepted my suit, he will not go against her."

"Very well. I had planned to attend the theater tomorrow evening. I will invite Penelope if you escort Miss Beauchamp."

Colin almost groaned aloud at the thought of having to spend an entire evening listening to Sybil's incessant chatter and simpering laughter.

It's only a means to an end, old boy ... and that end will see you wed to Penelope by the end of the Season.

"Very well," he agreed. "How goes the wife hunt? Any promising candidates yet?"

He glanced up at Edmond and found his friend leveling a blank stare at his shoes.

Shaking his head, Edmond sighed. "A few, though no one I feel excited about pursuing. Whoever she may be, I am running out of time."

"The Season has just begun," Colin argued.

"True," he agreed. "However, we both know the heiresses will be the first to go. I intend to make my selection and begin my pursuit of her by week's end."

Clapping his friend's shoulder, he tried to give him an encouraging smile. "Chin up, old boy. Your troubles are nearly at an end."

His response came out on a dry, harsh bark of laughter. "Colin, I have a feeling my troubles are only just begun."

Wrinkling his brow, he studied Edmond. What the devil could he mean by such a cryptic statement? He hated seeing Edmond—a man of good humor and even temperament—down in the doldrums.

Perhaps he referred to the possibility of a stale and loveless marriage, or the fact that said marriage would not solve all his money woes as long as the earl continued in his indulgences. Edmond might use her dowry to put his family's accounts in good standing, but if his father would not cease gambling away everything they owned, he might still inherit a bankrupt estate.

He had nothing to offer Edmond—his army wages were meager, and he only managed to live so well because of the allowance he received from his father every month. The best he could do was hope and pray that all would be well. If anyone deserved happiness and security, it was his best friend.

Penelope clapped one hand over her mouth, biting back the scream of anger and hurt burning in her chest. As it was, she found it difficult to control her breathing, which sawed in and out of her lungs noisily. She marveled at the fact that neither Colin nor Edmond could hear her, when she stood mere feet away from them, her heart pounding like a drum in her chest.

She'd abandoned Rose and Sybil, unable to abide such insipid conversation any longer. Deciding to remain behind had been a mistake, one that had trapped her with the two younger women as they whispered and giggled over how handsome Colin was.

"I could not believe it when he set his sights upon me," Sybil had sighed, her cheeks blushing a rosy pink. "Oh, and he's ever so polite and gallant. The perfect gentleman."

Penelope had suppressed a snort, wondering how the prim and proper little chit would feel if she knew that Colin's proper tongue had tasted her quim not long ago. The memory had only added fuel to the fire raging in her belly, causing her to feel as if her clothes fit too tight. Desire had mingled with anger, until she could hardly tell one emotion from the other.

Murmuring an excuse about stretching her legs, she had left before either could stop her, tramping off toward the trees in search of privacy. She had come upon Edmond and Colin, recognizing them both on sight, even from behind. Halting, she'd ducked behind a tree —more to escape being trapped alone with them than anything else. She'd held her breath, waiting for the lull in their conversation to end so she could walk away without them noticing her.

However, her name on Edmond's tongue had kept her frozen in place.

Penelope is seething with envy ...

She'd listened with a slack jaw as they'd discussed her so callously, as if she represented nothing more than a means to an end for them both. The audacity! The gall!

It became plain to her what their intent had been all along. Colin, not content to let matters lie after their first encounter, had enlisted Edmond's aid in manipulating her.

No, she realized suddenly, they'd been at it from the start. Remembering Edmond's insistence that she meet Colin in the garden during the Avonleah ball, Penelope felt anger turning her face hot. Together, they thought to influence her to their own ends. She knew what Colin's aim was. Of course he wanted her to be envious, so she'd come running to him as she had in the past, proving he still held power over her. That despite all the wrong he'd done, he could still use and control her with very little effort.

Adding insult to injury was the fact that he knew her so well. It had been working, as her envy of Sybil Beauchamp had been the very thing that had sent her into the woods in search of solitude.

But, what of Edmond? What did he seek to gain from aiding Colin? Perhaps it amused him to toy with her, or perhaps the two found satisfaction in exercising their prowess on the same unsuspecting female. Oh, Edmond had been the consummate actor, pretending to feel guilt over his attraction to her. But why? Perhaps, like Colin, he derived gratification from manipulating her into throwing herself at him.

Her teeth clenched so tight, it was a wonder they didn't break, and her hand curled into a fist.

If Colin and Edmond thought her the same naïve girl she had been three years ago, they were both sorely mistaken. It would seem time had taught them nothing, especially Colin.

With a smug smile, she decided there could be no better teacher. By the time she had finished, both men would be eating from her palm. And when all had been said and done, she'd walk away and leave them in the same state Colin had left her in all those years ago.

She'd long ago decided that no one would use her the way Colin had when he'd ruined her; yet, she had always treated her lovers with respect. After all, if two adults entered into a mutually satisfying arrangement, then secrecy, lies, and manipulation were not necessary.

However, she'd grown tired of it all. Men were animals, the lot of them, and had proven themselves to be good for nothing more than fulfilling her baser desires. It was time someone showed them how it felt to be tricked and subjugated. Nothing would bring her more pleasure than being the one to teach them this most valuable lesson.

CHAPTER 8

"You have been silent most of the evening," Edmond remarked from his side of the carriage. "Is everything all right? Did you not enjoy the theater?"

Seated across from him in the dark, Penelope fought back a smug smile. She had enjoyed their outing very much. When he'd first arrived at her family's townhouse to fetch her, she had met him in the foyer wearing a heavy black cloak over her ensemble. However, once ensconced in his family's theater box, free from the constraining garment, she had basked in his attention—as well as that of the men eyeing her from their vantage points.

The rose silk bodice clung to her breasts, the fabric made heavy by elaborate beading. Her breasts fought the confinement, pushed upward by her best corset. She'd detected Edmond's gaze straying toward her décolletage several times during the performance. In the box beside theirs, Colin had watched her when he assumed she would not notice, peering past both Sybil and her mother—who acted as their chaperone—to catch a glimpse of her. Despite having been angry with them for their duplicity, Penelope could not deny feeling both their lustful gazes on her at once had been thrilling, especially since neither of them was privy to her plans for them.

"I did," she replied, meeting his gaze with a smile. "It was a wonderful performance. I only wish ..."

Edmond perked up at the hesitation in her tone. "Yes?"

She shrugged one shoulder with an exaggerated motion, well aware that the movement caused her bosom to heave, barely held in place by her thin bodice and the slender cap sleeves of her gown. If she weren't mistaken, she detected the slight hitch of his breath.

"Well ... I enjoy spending time with you when we can talk. The theater does not leave very much room for conversation."

His white teeth gleamed in the near darkness, and he chuckled. "Well, that is what long carriage rides are for. What would you like to talk about, Penny?"

She leaned back against her seat and stretched her legs out, propping her feet up between his spread legs. He started, eyebrows lifting when he glanced up at her, but he offered no protest.

"How was your evening last night?" she asked. "What sort of raucous gentleman's pursuit did you indulge in?"

He laughed again. "I don't think this is a proper subject of conversation between an unmarried man and unmarried woman."

She pushed her lower lip out in a pout. "Drat. I thought we'd decided to become friends. I had hoped you could talk to me the same way you do our bosom beaus. Come on, Ed. We are alone. I am too far up on the shelf to need a chaperone, and you know how inane small talk sets my teeth on edge. What did you do?"

He grimaced, leaning forward and taking one of her feet in his. His fingers began massaging it through her thin slipper, exerting firm pressure. Sighing, she sank down in her seat further and waited for him to speak.

"I had dinner at White's with some acquaintances. It was hardly enjoyable, however. All I could think of was how much the meal was costing me, and how high all my unpaid account balances are. I could not stop glancing over my shoulder, waiting for the humiliating moment when I would be ejected and refused service."

Pity for him washed through her, leading her to almost feel guilty for what she was about do.

Like most men in his position, he will simply marry a wealthy heiress and use her dowry to line his pockets. He'll care nothing for the poor girl, whoever she happens to be.

His troubles would soon come to an end, and she intended to remain true to her word and help him find the right woman. However, there remained no reason she could not have her fun in the meantime.

"I apologize," she murmured. "I should not have asked."

He shrugged, still absently rubbing her foot. The pressure he applied to the arch sent bone-melting pleasure through her, ending with a lightning strike deep in her belly.

"How could you have known? It's all right. What of you?"

"Well," she murmured, lowering her gaze. "I elected to spend the evening at home and turn in early. Yet, once in my bed, I could not sleep."

He frowned. "You must be exhausted. You should have cried off for our outing tonight; I would have understood."

Sighing again, she straightened, removing her foot from his grasp. "I would not have missed our evening together for anything, Ed. Besides, there is a simple remedy for my affliction. It occurred to me as I lay tossing and turning all night ... I know exactly what is missing."

Leaning forward, elbows braced on his knees, he furrowed his brow. "Really? What?"

She smirked, finding amusement at his obliviousness. "A lover to keep me warm, of course. I haven't taken once since last Season, and I realize now it is the reason for my restlessness. I miss the feel of a man's strong arms around me, his lips on mine."

Edmond's jaw clenched, his lips pressing together as his nostrils flared. Yet, he did not release her gaze. His voice came out hoarse when he finally spoke.

"Penelope ... I don't think ... we shouldn't ..."

"Oh, I'm sorry," she replied. "I thought friends could discuss this sort of thing. I am helping you find a potential wife, am I not? Perhaps you could recommend a lover for me. Someone whose company I might enjoy for the span of the Season. Come now, Ed. I know the sort of conversations gentlemen have when there are no women about. You know which men possess the traits I am looking for."

"This is hardly appropriate, nor is it amusing."

He attempted to lecture her in a stern voice, but she could hear his uncertainty, as well as his harsh breath between words.

"But I am quite serious," she countered. "Tell me, Ed, where might I find a man who can make me laugh and engage me in stimulating conversation? Someone discreet, who might escort me to various engagements? Someone handsome with a pleasing physique?"

Jerking on his shirt collar, he avoided her gaze. "I am certain there are plenty—"

"I'm not finished yet," she admonished, pressing one finger to his lips.

His gaze grew heavy-lidded as she traced his lower lip, the silk of her glove teasing him before sliding lower to circle his chin.

"I need someone who isn't afraid to be a man. I am not a porcelain doll, and I do not relish being treated like one in bed. Someone who will master me, give me pleasure while also allowing me to lavish it on him. The sort of man who is not intimidated by a woman who is bold enough to state her needs quite clearly and does not play coy."

He took the finger of one of her gloves between his teeth and pulled, jerking his head to the side until it fell free. When she inched her finger toward his lips again, his tongue met it, laving the digit in a hot caress.

"A man who knows how to do wicked things with his tongue?" he whispered, kissing the tips of each finger, before brushing his lips against the inside of her wrist.

"Yes," she moaned as his tongue circled on the sensitive skin of her wrist while he swiftly removed her other glove.

He reached across the carriage and hauled her into his lap, not bothering to be gentle about it.

"How about a man with stamina ... one who would fuck you until you screamed and begged him to stop?"

"I would never—"

His lips, tracing a path up her throat, cut her off, stealing the air from her lungs.

"Sweetheart, when I'm done with you, you'll never want another man inside of you again. I am going to ruin you."

Tangling her fingers in his hair, she pulled, tilting his head back. His vibrant green eyes went dark, the pupils dilating in response to his state of arousal. Grinding her pelvis against his, she shuddered at the feel of his hard cock pressed against her mons. The raw power in the rigid organ made itself evident, even beneath the layers of his clothes.

"I have already been ruined, Edmond," she murmured, leaning into him until her breasts rested on his chest and their lips brushed. "I want you to conquer me."

Before, he'd been trembling, the hands holding her captive in his lap shaking as if he were unsure. She knew the moment he ceased holding back, his grip on her waist strong and sure as he swiftly reversed their positions, lurching across the carriage and depositing her on the opposite seat. He came down between her legs, his hips slamming against hers at the same moment his mouth claimed hers in a bruising kiss.

The bounce of the carriage left her feeling off-balance and out of control as he assaulted her mouth, his hands traveling up to tangle in her hair. There was nothing light or carefree about his kiss—its dominance at odds with his laid-back personality. He prodded her lips apart, then invaded her with his tongue, engaging her in a sensual dance of flesh. His teeth nipped at her lower lip, then he suckled it, chuckling at the sound of her surprised gasp.

Taking her chin in hand, he turned her head, trailing his tongue from her collarbone up to the point of her pulse, where he closed his lips and suckled before giving her another playful bite.

"You're a tease, Penelope," he declared, kneeling between her parted knees. "You want me? You'll have me … but on my terms. First, you're going to pay for driving me mad with desire."

Grinning at him, she arched her back as he gripped her bent knees, giving her a rough yank until her back met the seat of her carriage.

"What will my punishment be?" she asked, studying him from beneath lowered eyelids.

Without answering her, he removed his coat, turning to toss it on the opposite seat. Then, he removed his cravat, snatching it free with a rough jerk.

"First, I'm going to silence you," he grunted, twisting the cravat before lowering it between her lips, gagging her. "You talk too bloody much, and that naughty mouth of yours is going to get you in trouble someday."

A thrill ran through her as he urged her to lift her head before tying the cravat. The fabric felt rough against her tongue, but the realization that she enjoyed it flushed her cheeks with heat. No man had ever commanded her so thoroughly, and she was still fully clothed. Heat and moisture flooded her core as she imagined every filthy thing he might do to her while she lay in such a vulnerable position.

He nodded as if satisfied with his handiwork. Silently, he reached down and lifted her gown and petticoat, sucking in a sharp breath as he realized she wore no drawers.

"Christ," he muttered, palming her thighs and spreading them wide.

Lowering his head, he thrust his tongue between the lips of her pussy, drawing a strangled cry from her throat. It became trapped in her mouth by the gag, coming out as more of a whimper. Reaching down, she grasped his head and thrust her hips upward, urging him on.

Shrugging out of her hold, he sat upright, raising one dark eyebrow at her.

"No," he admonished, his tone gruff. "You are not in control here; I am. Listen to me and listen well. Keep those mischievous hands of yours to yourself if you want me to pleasure you. If we laid in my bed, I would tie you to the posts, so we are going to improvise. If you touch me without my permission, I will cease whatever I am doing immediately and you do not get to come. Understood?".

Whimpering from the longing he caused her body to feel, both with his words and his nearness, she nodded without hesitation, her eyes going wide. In the morning, she might wonder what she could be thinking to allow him to speak to her this way. However, at the moment, all that mattered was his promise of pleasure, the fulfillment of what she'd wanted from the moment he'd escorted her onto that ballroom floor for the quadrille.

Seeming satisfied with her response, he took her hands and spread them out to either side of her, laying them on the bench. Obeying his command, she kept them there as he lowered himself back between her thighs.

His long fingers parted the lips of her sex, baring her tender, intimate flesh to his view. He nudged her legs farther apart, until she was spread as far as could be. His thumb found her hidden nub, circling with gentle pressure. She moaned, the light touch making her hungry for more. He chuckled, clearly knowing his feather-light touch teased her as opposed to satisfying. Yet, he only increased pressure by a small degree, drawing a frustrated grunt from behind her gag.

He gave her an amused smirk, reaching up to snatch down her bodice while his thumb continued working between her nether lips. Giving one of her nipples a pinch, he smiled in satisfaction at her reaction—a shudder that wracked her body from head to toe. He rolled the hardened peak between his thumb and forefinger, then cupped her breast, kneading with a firm hand. The carriage lurched and he fell against her, his thumb applying just the right amount of pressure to her clit. She groaned, then sighed in satisfaction when he kept it up, pressing harder while stroking her in rapid circles.

Capturing one of her breasts between his lips, he suckled with deep pulls that seemed to intensify the throbbing between her thighs. He treated the other the same way, scraping the nipple with his teeth before taking it deep in his mouth. His tongue flicked her hardened tip in rapid circles, matching the rhythm of his fingers between her legs.

Her teeth clenched on the gag, her breasts heaving as she fought for air. His lips journeyed between her breasts, then upward, his tongue scorching its way up to her throat as he slid his forefinger into her sheath. He tickled her inner walls, teasing her as the digit thrust slowly in and out of her while his thumb continued circling her pearl.

She mumbled around the gag, but her words came out unintelligible.

"What's that, darling?" he murmured, giving her nipple another playful tweak. "Oh, if only you weren't gagged, you could tell me what you want. But you've been a bad girl, Penelope. You must learn your lesson. Now ... would you like another finger inside you? Is that what you want?"

She nodded, a whimper adding emphasis to her silent plea. Grinning, he obliged her, joining his solitary finger with a second, causing her to feel fuller and slightly more satisfied. She sighed in relief as he continued thrusting, his fingers caressing her channel with an undeniable expertise.

Lowering his head once more, he kissed her belly, circling her navel with his tongue.

"You're so wet, darling," he murmured, dipping lower and nuzzling her mons, his breath tickling her. "Shall I taste you again?"

She could only moan behind her gag and raise her hips, hoping it would urge him on without violating his rules.

Apparently, movement of any kind was unacceptable. Clicking his tongue in admonishment, he pulled her further down the bench, until her hips hung off completely and her feet rested on the floor.

Reaching beneath her, he gripped one cheek of her buttocks, giving it a squeeze before following it with a slap. She gasped as the sound echoed through the conveyance, and the sting mingled with the pleasure he'd stoked as he slid his fingers back inside her. Fire burned where his hand had made contact, yet she hovered maddeningly close to climax with his fingers taking up a swift thrust inside her.

"Hold still, or I'll be forced to do that again," he chided.

His hand beneath her continued massaging her arse, rubbing away the sting. Despite him dubbing what he'd done a 'punishment,' she found herself wistfully missing the pain. However, she wanted what would come next more than she did another swat on her backside.

His tongue found her cunt again, massaging her wet inner folds with a slow up and down motion. She dug her heels into the floor and fought not to move her hips in time with his tongue strokes. She heard his groan of pleasure, felt the sound vibrate from his mouth to her vulnerable flesh. The hum only heightened her arousal and desire —knowing he enjoyed this as much as she did gave her a sense of power despite her position as a submissive partner. Edmond might be in control, but even now, he could not deny his own need. The evidence of it had been pressed against her just a few short minutes ago.

His lips closed around her pearl, drawing it into his hot mouth. Penelope screamed, unable to halt the jolt of her hips as her back bowed in response to the intense pleasure. The hand cupping her buttocks fell away, then came against the flesh with an impact that left her reeling. Lifting his head, he stared up at her, his fingers quickening inside of her.

"Now, Penny," he whispered. "You have my permission to come."

Relief flooded her, and she closed her eyes as he took her clit between his lips once more, suckling with hungry pulls while his fingers thrust hard and swift, mimicking what she wished for him to do to her with his cock.

Her eyes watered, her chest expanding with the breath she held as she strained toward her impending climax. When it came in pounding waves, she released her breath on a moan, squirming and writhing in his hold.

Grasping her thighs, he spread them even wider, until her knees rested on the seat. His fingers dug into her flesh, and she did not doubt he left fingerprints. As she floated down from her thunderous completion, he soothed her with his tongue. Lapping at her gently, and suckling so lightly, she thought his tenderness might kill her. Once the spasms had stilled, she fell limp, and Edmond straightened.

Tearing his waistcoat and shirt open, he took her hands and placed them upon the flat, ridged plane of his abdomen.

"Touch me," he rasped, his voice gone heavy and thick from desire.

She obliged him readily, running her hands up to his chest, then outward to flick her fingers over his nipples. Groaning, he leaned over her, his mouth caressing her throat, up to her jaw while he lifted her head to remove the gag. Smoothing her hands around his shoulders, she scored her fingernails down his back, then reached down and grasped his buttocks, pulling him flush against her. Through his breeches, she could feel his arousal—long, thick, and rock hard.

Reaching between them, she tore at the fastening of his breeches to open them, yanking down his drawers to free his cock. He moaned as she stroked him, then reached down and showed her how he wanted it, urging her to tighten her grip.

"Ah, yes, that's it … God's teeth, you have beautiful hands."

She reached down to palm his bollocks, causing his hips to surge and a hiss to escape from between his teeth. There could be no denying she enjoyed exacting revenge for the torment he'd inflicted. Adding satisfaction was the fact that it came so easy.

Seeming to sense that she'd wrested control from him, he took her hand and snatched it away, raising it above her head. Taking the other, he repeated the action, then crossed her wrists, capturing them both in one hand. With his other, he reached down and palmed his cock.

Penelope licked her lips at the sight of him stroking his erection, the powerful organ begging to be sheathed inside of her, a pearlescent bead of his seed seeping from the slit. He caught the drop with his thumb, smearing it over his head, before edging closer.

"If we had more time, I would place my cock between those beautiful lips. I would kiss every inch of you, right down to your pretty toes. I'd tie you to my bed facedown and fuck your tight little arse."

She shivered at the thought of that thick organ entering her rear passage. The most she'd ever experienced with her past lovers had been a finger prodding the tight channel. She'd always wondered how it would feel to have a man enter her that way, yet had held back from trying it with her other paramours. With Edmond, she just knew it would be wonderful.

"But for now ... I'll have to settle for a hard and fast fuck. Next time, though ..." he paused, giving her the lopsided grin she'd come to know so well. "Next time, I am going to fuck you every way I can think of ... then I'll create a new way, and another, and another."

He thrust his hips, allowing his cock to tease her inner folds and clit. She gasped, raising her hips toward his, urging him to do it again.

Still fisting his cock, he laid it between her lips and thrust again, this time creating more friction. They groaned in unison, the sounds mingling together. She gazed down to where their bodies joined, watching him disappear, then reappear between her lips, his swollen head glistening from her juices.

"Oh," she whimpered "Oh, Edmond ..."

The pressure in her groin built again, little effort needed to stoke her back toward completion when her flesh remained so sensitive to every touch.

"Do you wish to come again, love?"

She nodded, forgetting that he had removed the cravat.

He braced himself on his elbows over her, still steadily moving against her, the smooth slide of his cock against her swollen clit causing little flutters to indicate she hovered near the edge.

"Ask me ... ask me for what you want."

"Edmond," she gasped, wrapping her legs around his waist and digging her heels into his lower back.

Still, he held back, waiting for the words.

"I want to come, Edmond," she pleaded. "Please!"

"Good girl," he murmured against her ear.

His pace accelerated, the pressure increasing as he grasped her hips and held her more tightly against him. She buried her face in his shoulder, muffling her screams as the small tremors gave way to throbbing pulsations that echoed through her entire being. His hoarse groans increased as she grew wetter, soaking him in her essence. As the spasms died away, Edmond pulled back and slammed into her, finally joining his body to hers.

Hooking his arms beneath her knees, he lifted her lower body, tilting her to the perfect angle as he pounded her so hard, it became impossible to draw breath. The dying climax roared to life again, causing her cries of delirious pleasure to die in her throat. She was capable of no more than strangled gasps as he dominated her, mastered her, showed her what her body was truly capable of.

Every muscle in his body tensed as a light sheen of sweat gleamed on the surface of his skin. The tendons in his neck strained, his teeth gritting as he grunted and groaned, his breath racing as his pace increased even more, an impossible feat proven possible in the blink of an eye.

He was right … the pleasure had grown so intense now, pleas for mercy hovered on the tip of her tongue. Yet, it felt too damned good to stop now, an exquisite torture too hard to bear, yet impossible to refuse.

Her final scream of release blended with his bellow as he jerked and groaned, then pulled free of her sheath.

The warm gush of his seed spread across her belly and he fell against her, his face buried in her neck. Lying beneath him, Penelope became too weak to move, and far too sated to protest his heavy weight.

After a moment, he seemed to realize he crushed her and righted himself. Reaching into his breast pocket, he produced a handkerchief, using it to clean her. Then, he closed her legs and pulled her skirts down to her ankles. Tucking his cock back into his drawers, he fastened his breeches, then helped her sit upright and pull her bodice back over her exposed breasts.

Easing onto the seat beside her, he took her into his arms, his hands gentle between her shoulders and the back of her neck. She sighed when he kissed her, the movement of his lips over hers languid and tender. The moment dragged on, with him drinking from her mouth as if she held his last breath, until the carriage rolled to a halt before her residence.

"We've arrived," she murmured as he reluctantly drew away.

His thumb caressed her lower lip. "So we have. I know there should be something else … guilt, perhaps. But all I can bring myself to feel at the moment is satisfaction. Being with you … inside you … it was everything I knew I would be. Then it was more."

"I feel the same way," she replied, reaching out to touch his face. "There is no place for guilt in my bed, Edmond. Only pleasure and satisfaction, friendship. Three things you and I seem to have no problem with. Agreed?"

He gave her his radiant smile, and the sight of it caused a sensation in her chest, not unlike a tight squeeze.

"Agreed," he murmured just as the carriage door swung open.

He descended before her, turning to offer his hand. From where he stood, dressed in his evening finery with the moonlight caressing him, he appeared the perfect picture of a gentleman. Only she knew the debauched and spine-tinglingly delicious things he was capable of.

Allowing him to hand her down from the carriage, she hoped she appeared as unruffled as he did. Tucking her hand into the crook of his arm, he led her up the stairs to her front door.

Turning to face her, he lifted her hand to his lips. His kiss was chaste on her knuckles, yet the glittering gaze he fixed upon her was anything but.

"Thank you for a most … stimulating evening, my lady. We must do it again, soon."

As her front door opened to reveal the butler waiting for her,

Penelope was forced to turn and go inside, carrying her memories of Edmond up the stairs and to her bedroom, where she collapsed onto the bed with a wide smile across her face.

One man down, one left. Take care, Captain ... if Edmond crumbled so easily, you don't stand a chance!

CHAPTER 9

Alone in his carriage, Edmond slouched in the seat and stared off into the darkness with unseeing eyes. Despite the satisfaction sexual release had brought him, his mind remained turbulent, thoughts of both Colin and Penelope robbing him of the pleasure he ought to be experiencing reliving the explosive encounter.

Colin wanted to wed Penelope, and while Edmond knew she felt attraction for him, he wasn't foolish enough to believe he could compete. In the end, his friend would win, and Penelope would become his wife. And he … he was a bloody idiot. While they married and lived out their days in comfort and happiness, he would be trapped with the guilt of knowing he had broken the most sacred rule of friendship between men. A kiss might have been forgiven, but this … this went beyond anything that could be pardoned. He hadn't just fucked Penelope; he had done so with an almost callous sort of satisfaction, and very little thought to the consequences.

At least, he had stopped just short of spilling his seed inside her, a decision that had taken a great deal of effort. Pulling out of that tight, wet sheath had proved one of the hardest things he'd ever done in his life.

Even after she had left, her scent remained—feminine arousal mingled with some sort of rose oil. Closing his eyes, he inhaled, unable to stop himself from picturing her spread out on the carriage seat, her eyes heavy-lidded with desire. Just the thought brought his cock to life again, causing it to grow thick and painful, throbbing with a need only she could satisfy.

It was the single, most idiotic thing he could have done, because he could not pretend it would not happen again. He'd all but promised her it would, despite the fact that he had been recruited to help Colin win her over to his side. Now, he found himself torn between his best friend and a woman he desired more than he'd ever wanted anyone.

It's only for a short time, he told himself.

He must wed someone with money by Season's end, and if he hadn't missed his guess, Colin would have successfully snared Penelope by then. Despite their physical connection, he knew she loved his best friend and had never stopped … even if she did not yet realize it. A few months of enjoyment and no one ever had to know, save he and Penelope. He supposed she would deal with the remorse in her own way, and he would do the same.

This was how it would have to be, because he couldn't possibly tell Colin the truth, nor could he resist the magnetic pull he felt toward Penelope. Even if he could have fought it, he knew deep down that he did not wish to. Being with her had felt too bloody good.

Colin descended the front steps of Worthing House and smiled, a feeling of excitement washing over him at the sight of his belongings being carted away in wagons, several footmen accompanying it. Tonight, he would sleep in his own bed for the first time since returning from Belgium. His injury had required constant care, and his mother had insisted he receive it under her roof. While he loved his family, being the third son had taught him to value solitude and independence. His elder brother, Wesley, would inherit the title, and fill Worthing House with a wife and children someday. He never wished to be underfoot when that day came, so he'd taken rooms in one of the many gentlemen's lodging at St James Place. While life in his family home was decidedly more luxurious, there was something to be said for living in one's own residence, no matter how small it might be.

Besides, at the moment, he only required enough space for himself and his valet. If he had his way, the end of the Season would change things, after which he looked forward to securing a townhouse for himself and Penelope—one large enough for them and a growing brood. The idea brought a smile to his face as he recalled the picnic at Richmond Park with a great deal of amusement.

He hadn't needed Edmond to inform him that Penelope had grown jealous over his association with Sybil Beauchamp. He knew her well, able to detect the subtle facial expressions representing her various emotions. The problem remained that while she might be jealous, her pride would never allow her to admit it. His mission would eventually become wooing her until she cracked, because he could accept no other outcome. Penelope would be his, forever, the ugliness of their past left behind them once and for all.

"I certainly hope your departure is not a sign that you intend to resume your old scapegrace behaviors."

Biting back a scathing retort, he turned to find that Wesley had joined him on the front steps, dressed for driving. Avoiding Colin's gaze, he watched as his phaeton was brought around, taking the place of the departed wagons.

"Of course not," he replied, knowing his brother's concerns over his behavior were not completely unfounded.

However, he wished everyone could see that his time in the army had changed him. He was he libertine third son of a viscount no longer.

"My living situation is only temporary, at any rate," he continued. "I intend to be married by Season's end."

Wesley turned to face him, one eyebrow raised. "Really? Any

particular chit in mind? I've heard you're spending a lot of time with Miss Sybil Beauchamp. That would be a fine match, Colin. She's a beautiful young woman, and comes from a good family. Not a wealthy heiress, but her dowry is adequate. Managed well along with your army pay and allowance, you could form quite a comfortable life with her. It is the sensible thing to do."

Colin's jaw ticked in annoyance. He knew Wesley only mentioned Sybil to discourage him from pursuing Penelope. As the heir, he had always been a stickler for propriety. If at all possible, he'd been angrier about his error with Penelope than even their father.

"Miss Beauchamp is only one of many options I intend to explore. Never worry, the lady I marry will come from a good family, but not so good as to compete with whoever your future viscountess happens to be."

Wesley's nostrils flared as he fought to keep his expression passive. "Colin, whatever you are up to, I strongly advise you to cease. You ruined any chance you might have had with Lady Penelope three years ago, and anything you do now could only call more attention to you both and incite the scandal we worked so hard to cover up in the first place. Do not make a fool of Father by disgracing our name. If you do, when he asks me what is to be done about you, I will do everything I can to convince him you are to be disowned."

As his own vehicle arrived behind Wesley's, he tightened his grip on his walking stick and leveled his coolest stare at his brother.

"I realize that you have a certain responsibility as the heir, and your first obligation is to our family and your reputation. However, allow me to make you privy to something. Your name and cold stare might intimidate lesser men, Wes, but you do not frighten me. Not any longer. Not since I went to war and learned what it is to stare death in the eye, to smell my own blood as it leaves my body, to hear the cries of dying men. I have faced far greater foes, and received the honor of Captain before my name—not by running or cowering, but by fighting. While you were here before the fire with your port and cozy sense of entitlement, I was freezing my bollocks off in Belgium, lying in wait for my enemy to come and kill me. So, I say again, you do not frighten me in the least. If you feel you must punish me for my slights—past, present, or imagined—then you go right ahead. Do your worst."

Without waiting for a response, Colin descended the steps, climbing onto the perch of his gig. Wesley's stony gaze followed him as he took up the reins, but Colin ignored him.

He had a pleasant afternoon planned at Gentleman Jackson's, where Edmond had promised to meet him for sparring. Afterward, he would escort Sybil on a ride through Hyde Park, where he hoped to encounter Penelope.

Tipping his hat to his fuming brother, he gave the reins a snap and went on his way.

"Her."

Edmond followed the discreet tilt of Penelope's head to the small cluster of ladies striding in their direction. There were three, each one with plain, milky faces and bodies draped in childish lace and frills.

"Dear God, please tell me you're referring to someone *behind* them."

Despite their unfortunate appearances, she had it on good authority that each of these women came endowed with large dowries. However, there was one particular chit she had in mind for him.

Smiling, she gave his bicep a light squeeze. They strolled together in Hyde Park, the perfect place for him to engage potential mates in conversation.

"Now, now, Edmond. Be good. The lady in the middle ... Cassandra Lane. She is perfect for you. Young, but not too young; this is her second season. A marquis' daughter with quite a hefty dowry. She's also quite shy and demure. With your charm, you'll capture her interest in an instant."

Sighing, he fixed a smile on his face—a lazy movement of his lips she had come to recognize as his public façade. It was nothing like the private smile he gave her when they found themselves alone.

"I'd much rather drag you behind the nearest shrub, throw you down on your hands and knees, and mount that beautiful arse of yours. But … if you insist."

His words caused her cheeks to grow hot as she imagined the scenario. "I thought I told you to be good."

Arching a dark eyebrow at her, he smirked. "Very well. I'll be good … for the nonce."

Plastering her best social smile upon her face, she led him toward the approaching ladies. "Miss Chadwick, Miss Lane, Miss Beecham," she said to all three. "How lovely it is to see you this afternoon. Have you had the opportunity to meet Lord Ingham?"

Cassandra Lane's cheeks flushed as Edmond turned the full force of his wicked smile upon her.

"The pleasure is all mine," he murmured, executing an elegant bow.

"While you become acquainted, I believe I shall go over and greet Captain Worthing and Miss Beauchamp. I'll return shortly."

Edmond nodded in response, going back to Miss Lane, while Penelope walked toward Colin and Sybil, who strolled at a leisurely pace on the opposite side of the path. The sight of the young chit's arm linked through Colin's set her teeth on edge, but she forced a smile as she waved in greeting, hailing them from her side of the path.

"Oh, Captain Worthing, Miss Beauchamp! How lovely it is to see you this afternoon."

They paused, moving aside from the other walkers to meet her in the middle of the lane. Sybil's smile was radiant as she released Colin's arm.

"Good afternoon, Lady Penelope. Isn't the weather just perfect today? My, don't you look lovely!"

Penelope skirted a glance toward Colin, who watched her with curious eyes. She fought back a smirk as she noticed the slight tick of his jaw, and the spasm of one hand at his side. His discomfiture brought her a smug sense of satisfaction.

"Thank you, Miss Beauchamp, you are looking well. Captain, good afternoon."

Colin cleared his throat and joined them, edging toward her as if she were a lioness who might maul him at any moment.

"My lady, how do you fare this afternoon?"

She extended her gloved hand to him with a smile, careful to keep the slip of paper she hid against her palm in place using her thumb. Shock briefly flickered across Colin's face at her pleasant tone, but he recovered quickly and took her hand. He seemed to feel the note in her palm, his gaze darting up to meet hers as he bent to kiss the air above her knuckles. He curled his fingers around the note just before releasing her hand.

"I am well, thank you," she replied. "Now, do excuse me. I am walking with Lord Ingham, and I must get back to him. Enjoy the rest of your afternoon."

She gave Colin a coy smile as she backed away, then turned to find Edmond. His gaze followed, hot on her back. Approaching Edmond and Miss Lane, she found them parting ways, as well. Offering her his arm once again, he led her along the path, continuing in their previous direction.

"Well?" she prodded. "How did it go?"

He shrugged. "Well enough, I suppose. I secured a dance with her at Almack's this evening."

She nodded, glancing back over her shoulder to find Cassandra and her friends giggling and darting glances at him.

"A step in the right direction. Her behavior indicates that she is already besotted with you. Dance a bit of attention upon her this Season, and you'll secure a betrothal agreement in no time. A summer wedding at St. George's, a wedding trip to the country ..."

"Sounds thrilling," he remarked, his tone dry. "Shall I see you at Almack's tonight? It'll be far more interesting with you there. I can whisper naughty words to you during a few dances, and take you home at the end of the night. I could tuck you in."

While she hated Almack's and had not attended an assembly since her first Season, his end of the night proposal would have coaxed her into suffering through it if she did not already have evening plans.

"I'm sorry, darling," she murmured. "I already have plans for the night.

"Then forget Almack's," he replied. "Tell me what time you intend to return home. Leave your window open for me, and I'll come to you."

Her breath hitched, her nipples hardening beneath her walking dress at the thought of Edmond appearing over her windowsill, hair tousled by an evening breeze, eyes smoldering with lust for her. Just the idea of him fucking her with her parents just down the hall sent a shiver of excitement down her spine. Perhaps he'd even gag her again to keep her quiet.

You are in control here, not Edmond, she reminded herself.

He and Colin had thought to manipulate her, but she would not allow them. Her encounters with Edmond would happen on her terms, not his.

"Tomorrow night," she decided. "I have no notion of when we might return. I wouldn't want to keep you waiting."

Approaching one of the park entrances, they exited out onto the sidewalk, Edmond turning them in the direction of her home.

"Fine, then. But I *will* punish you for making me wait, Penelope, so you may as well prepare yourself."

A slow pulsation began between her thighs in anticipation. Her face grew hot at the thought of Edmond's large palm smacking her arse as he had in the carriage. If that was the sort of punishment he had in mind, Penelope decided keeping him waiting might just be the smartest idea she'd ever had.

CHAPTER 10

olin paced back and forth before the small hearth in his sitting room, hands clasped tight behind his back. In the pocket of his breeches, Penelope's note settled with the weight of stone boulder, burning with all the intensity of a hot coal. He'd read it enough times that the words seemed indelibly seared into his memory.

C,

I think we have avoided the inevitable long enough. I can no longer pretend you do not exist, when it is clear we have unfinished business between us. Let us cease with games, and be honest with one another. I believe we want the same thing. I will visit you at home this evening to discuss it further.

Yours,

P

The hope her words gave him could not be squelched. Penelope knew he had marriage on his mind … what else could she mean by asserting that they wanted the same thing? He smiled to think that his strategy had worked. Perhaps seeing him with Sybil had caused her to realize that he belonged with her. And thank the heavens for that.

Sybil was a lovely young woman, but he could not picture himself with her permanently. She possessed none of Penelope's passion and fire, and not an ounce of her intelligence or wit.

The sooner he secured Penelope's promise of forever, the sooner he could move forward with planning their future. At the moment, everything had ground to a standstill, as he felt there could be no forward movement without her.

A knock sounded at his door, and he took a deep breath, forcing himself to take his time answering it. After their encounter at the Avonleah's ball, where she'd humiliated him, he'd realized the need to act aloof. If she saw weakness in him, she would pounce upon him like a cat mauling a mouse.

Swinging the door open with deliberate slowness, he revealed her shrouded in a black cloak, which disguised her identity. Yet, he'd have recognized her anywhere as she swept past him and into his flat without a word. He closed the door and turned to find she faced him, lowering the hood to reveal herself. The flames in the hearth set her auburn locks on fire and left an amber glow on her cheeks.

"Thank you for meeting with me," she murmured, returning his gaze without a blink.

"Thank you for coming. Though, if you wanted to speak, I would have come to you. I would not want someone to see you coming here in the dead of night alone."

He expected a well-timed barb from Penelope over his concern about her reputation. Instead, she smiled.

"I am not new to intrigues, Colin. Besides, I took great care that no one saw or followed me. Perhaps next time, you may come to me."

He raised his eyebrows, unable to hide his shock. "Next time?"

Reach up to unclasp her cloak, she allowed it to fall at her feet, revealing the simple white gown she wore beneath it, and the swell of her breasts against the décolletage.

"Surely, you must know why I have come," she purred, one hand resting on her hip.

"Yes, to talk," he replied, meeting her at the center of the room.

A sensual smirk curved her mouth, and a twinkle of mischief alit in her gaze. "We can talk after."

Realizing her intent, he clenched his hands into fists at his side, fighting the urge to assist her as she lifted her hands to her coiffure and begin removing the pins. The first lock of hair fell free, tumbling over her shoulder and curling decorously against her left breast.

"Penelope—"

"You were right, Colin," she interjected. "We were so good together, and my need for you has been harder to put aside than I thought."

She tossed her handful of hair pins onto the nearby end table, then moved her hands to the back of her dress. His pulse began to throb at the base of his throat as her gown became looser while she flicked the buttons from their holes.

Need, she'd said. Her *need* of him.

Battling the urge to pinch himself, he recalled that this was real. Penelope had arranged this meeting, and he did not dream it.

She continued, still working to unbutton her gown. "Seeing you with that ... that *girl* ..."

"I never laid a hand on her," he insisted. "I never wanted to. All I've ever wanted is you."

Colin forgot he was supposed to be playing at aloofness. With her standing there, saying she needed him, he forgot everything other than just how much he needed her as well.

"Good," she replied, pulling one arm free from her dress, then the other, allowing the garment to hang from her hips.

She wore no undergarments, and the sight of her pink nipples sent a heated surge of blood straight to his groin.

"Show me, Colin," she murmured, her hands tracing a path up from her hips, over her belly and ribs, up to the luscious tits begging for his touch. "Show me how badly you want me."

A lump lodged itself in his throat, making speech difficult. Still, he persevered, determined to say what needed to be said.

"I want to," he admitted. "But we should ... There is so much uncertain between us. I'm afraid if I lose myself in you right now, I'll never say the things I need to say to you."

"Why tell me when you can demonstrate it to me so easily?" she replied, her voice hitching on a moan as she kneaded her breasts, her thumbs and forefingers teasing the nipples into stiff peaks.

His cock swelled, throbbing from the pulsation of blood filling the thick vein along its side. His mouth went dry as she continued touching herself, tilting her head back and sighing.

"I want your hands on me, Colin ... your lips ... your wicked tongue. Will you deny me?"

Flexing his fingers, he took another step toward her, drawn by her magnetic pull. "No," he rasped, his voice gone husky and thick.

She gasped, pinching her nipple a bit harder, while her other hand snaked beneath the gown still hanging from her hips. His gaze lowered to the hand moving beneath the white fabric, only able to guess at what she might be doing that caused her cheeks to flush pink and her lips to part on another moan.

Closing the remaining distance between them, he grasped her waist with one hand and took hold of the wrist dipping beneath her clothes. Withdrawing her busy hand, he brought it to his lips, finding her fingers soaked in the evidence of her arousal. The scent of her caused his head to swim and his cock to twitch in his breeches, as if fighting for freedom. He pressed the erection against her, grinding it against the soft cradle between her thighs. Bringing her glistening digits to his lips, he took them into his mouth, stroking them with his tongue and tasting her sweet honey. He moaned at the taste of her, feminine and sweet.

She wrapped her arms around him, pressing her face against his neck, her lips skimming the vital vein supplying his pulse. Her hot tongue flicked out to taste it, sending a tremor down his spine. Reaching down into the garment, he palmed her buttocks, kneading the plump cheeks and pressing her closer to him. The friction of her pelvis against his proved nearly unbearable, reminding him that it had been far too long since he'd found release any other way than by his own hand.

He lifted her, and she jumped, wrapping her legs around his waist as he carried her further into the sitting room. She held on to his shoulders tight as he went to his knees, then lay her down onto the rug before the fire. Kneeling before her, he finished undressing her, removing the gown, then her slippers and stockings.

He crouched between her legs then, taking a moment to simply look at her. Imagining her this way so many times hadn't prepared him, and he found himself unable to take his eyes off her.

"Christ, you're beautiful," he murmured, stroking along her bare thigh with the tips of his fingers. "I don't think I truly appreciated just how much until I had to go day after day without seeing you. I'd forgotten what beauty was until I found you again."

For a moment, she did not respond—she didn't even move. He heard her breath catch and hold, and her eyes widened as if his words had taken her by surprise. Yet, he couldn't find it in himself to feel sorry for disarming her that way. It was the truth, and he'd promised himself after returning home that he would only speak the truth to Penelope. Lies had nearly destroyed them.

Finally, she smiled, her hand skimming her stomach once more and finding its way between her legs. Stroking herself, she seemed to derive satisfaction from his reaction, her gaze falling to the growing organ making itself evident against the front his breeches.

Lowering his head, he kissed one ankle, taking his time as he made his way further up. She trembled beneath him when his lips skimmed her calf, then dipped down to her inner thigh. She cried out when he bit her, taking a good bit of flesh between his teeth, then soothed it with a few strokes of his tongue.

Her hands grasped his head, fingers tangling in his hair as she coaxed him higher, urging him on. Resting his head against her thigh, he delved his index finger between the cheeks of her buttocks, tickling the entrance. She gasped, hips bucking as he continued teasing her, bringing his thumb against her pearl. Stroking it in slow circles, he lifted his gaze to watch her reaction to his every touch. He nibbled the inside of her thigh, working his way inward with slow tongue strokes. While prodding her sheath with his thumb, his finger gained an inch into her rear passage, causing her eyes to widen in shock. He grinned at the thought that he'd created a new sensation for her, realizing her response had changed from one of shock to one of delight. Keeping his stare locked on her face, he dipped his head and flicked his tongue out, stroking the throbbing bud of her clit, once. The sensation of her intimate flesh upon his tongue proved far more decadent than anything he'd ever tasted. The single lap drew a sharp gasp, then a low moan from her. Her hips raised in response, but he regained control of her, lowering them to the floor while continuing on his way up her body.

Penelope squirmed as he trailed his tongue along her naked skin, tracing a circle around her hip bone, then following the curve of her waist. His hands preceded him now, skimming her ribs before cupping her breasts and giving her nipples a light pinch. Following his hands with his tongue, he reveled in the mewls of pleasure he coaxed from her as his tongue traced rapid circles around one nipple before he drew it into his mouth and suckled with deep, ravenous pulls. The hardened bud of her nipple caressed his tongue in response, her soft flesh filling his mouth, goosebumps breaking out over her skin in response.

Soft sighs escaped her throat while he kissed his way steadily upward, his lips caressing her breastbone, tongue skimming one collarbone, then dipping into the hollow between it and her neck. Her back arched, pressing the plush mounds of her breasts against his chest as she clawed at him, her fingernails caressing his chest through the open vee of his shirt, tickling the light blond coils smattered over his skin.

She grasped his collar and pulled, tearing several buttons loose and sending them rolling across the floor. Shrugging out of the shirt, Colin continued his exploration, stroking her pulse point with his tongue before giving the side of her neck a light but firm bite. She cried out, hips bucking against his, fingernails sinking into his shoulder. He groaned at the pleasure of it, mingled with pain. His valet would likely find the imprint of her nails across his back, but he could not bring himself to care. Angling his mouth over the line of her jaw and inching toward her lips, he vowed to have her clawing him like a wildcat before the end.

Stiffening, she turned her head before he could kiss her lips, bowing her back once more as if to offer her breasts instead. The sting of her rejection could not be ignored, nor could the urge to taste her mouth. It had grown even stronger now that he'd realized they had not kissed once since his return.

Taking her earlobe between his teeth, he caressed it with his tongue, then kissed her neck just beneath it.

"It's all right," he whispered, nuzzling her neck, inhaling the scent of her hair. "You can trust me, Penelope ... with every part of you. You don't have to wear your armor with me. Let me love you."

Staring up at him, she blinked as if holding back tears, lower lip disappearing between her teeth. She trembled, her hands clutching his biceps tight, legs wrapped around his waist.

"I'm not holding back," she whispered, her voice unsteady.

He smiled, dipping his head until his hair brushed her brow. "Yes, you are. But that's all right. I'll show you what you mean to me, if it's the last thing I do ... until not a glimmer of a doubt exists in your mind."

Opening his breeches, he angled himself toward her opening. He gritted his teeth as the feel of her—hot, wet, and pulsating— enveloped him inch by slow inch. Pausing, he closed his eyes, fighting for control. It had been far too long since he'd been inside a woman, and climax would come within a few strokes if he weren't careful.

Grasping his shoulders, Penelope turned them until he lay on his back with her astride his hips, still wrapping him in her tight sheath. He groaned, his chest burning as he released the breath he'd been holding. Opening his eyes, he fought not to allow the pleasure to overwhelm him as she slid up and down his cock, her juices soaking him, her velvety walls squeezing him in a fist-tight grip.

"Ah, Penelope," he grunted, grasping her hips and attempting to slow her movements. "Slow down, love ... it's been too long. I'm going to ... Goddamn it!"

Resting her hands on his chest, she rotated her hips, ignoring his plea and moving faster, bouncing her luscious arse against his thighs in a rhythm that stole his breath. Realizing he would not last much longer, he reached between them and stroked between her nether lips until finding her clit. Rubbing in rapid circles, he pressed down, eliciting a sharp scream from her.

Urging her on toward climax, he met her thrusts with his own, bracing his feet against the floor and undulating in time with her movements. Still steadily stroking her clit, he reached up with his free hand and grasped one breast, massaging it while tweaking the nipple with his fingers. A rush of moisture seeped from her core, drenching his cock and bollocks, and slickening the path inside of her even more. Colin's strokes now penetrated so deep, he wondered if he'd ever find his way out again. As her channel tightened around him, and she collapsed on top of him with a shrill cry, he decided he did not want to.

He pumped into her a few more times before grasping her waist and lifting her off of him just before spending. His seed spilled out of him in a hot rush, cascading over his cock and wetting his stomach.

Breathing a sigh of relief, he allowed his head to fall back onto the rug as what remained of his energy fled.

He could have stayed there all night, sleeping on the floor until morning. Yet, he became aware that Penelope was leaving him, kneeling beside him and beginning to stand. He attempted to reach for her, but allowed her to go once it became evident that she had weakened him considerably.

Colin opened his eyes and watched her pad across the room, nude, to his bedchamber. Despite the amount of time it had been, he realized she remembered her way around his flat. She returned, carrying a damp towel, which she placed in his hand. Cleaning himself, he watched her crouch to take up her chemise, which she pulled on while he quickly fastened his breeches, concealing his cock and the ugly scars reaching up from his thigh toward his groin. He'd remained partially dressed to hide the deformity. He had defenses of his own, which would remain in place until he felt certain Penelope was coming to love him again.

Rising to a seated position, he gazed up at her with a sheepish grin.

"If you would be so kind," he murmured, extending one arm toward her. "My leg."

An expression he read as pity creased her brow as she approached him, taking his hand. She pulled, assisting him to his feet. Before she could move away from him again, he snaked an arm around her waist and drew her up against his body.

Her protest melted away when he kissed her neck, teasing her with a few playful nips. She went pliant in his arms, her body sinking into his.

"That was most certainly worth the wait," he murmured.

She drew back and stared up at him, lips parted, eyes narrowed. "You really were telling the truth about that, weren't you?"

"Was it the almost instant climax that clued you in?" he quipped. "If you give me a moment, I'll be ready for another go … and I promise it will last longer than five minutes this time."

Penelope giggled at that, pressing a hand to his chest to push him away. Plopping down onto his sofa, she crossed one leg over the other, baring her calves. Colin resisted the urge to fall at her feet and busy his hands beneath her chemise until his cock could rise to the occasion again. Already, his groin pooled with blood as desire grew within him once more. While he wanted her again, he meant to hold her to her word that they would talk after lovemaking.

Striding to the sideboard, he retrieved a snifter of brandy and two tumblers. After splashing a bit into each one, he took them up and joined her on the sofa, offering her one. She accepted it, humming with appreciation as she took a little sip of the liquor. He followed suit, leaning against the back of the sofa and closing his eyes as the warmth of the spirits raced down his throat and chest before blossoming in his belly.

"Of course I was telling the truth," he mumbled without opening his eyes. "There were women aplenty, everywhere I went, many willing to part their legs for a soldier. But there is only one woman who can satisfy me, Penelope, and that woman is you. You ruined me."

Her voice came out a low whisper. "And here I thought *you* had ruined *me*."

Sitting up, he turned his head to meet her gaze, elbows rested on his knees with the glass held between his fingers.

"It would seem you have thrived in my absence. There isn't a man in a London who wouldn't give his two front teeth to claim you, and in a few months, you'll become one of the wealthiest women among the *ton*. As much as we all want you, the fact remains you have no more need of us than you do a sole-less shoe … and well you know it. It only makes us covet you more."

Penelope arched one eyebrow at him, taking another sip of her brandy. "Is that why you've been courting Sybil Beauchamp? Because she is more … needy?"

He grimaced, staring down at the amber liquid in his tumbler before taking a healthy swallow. "You told me to turn my attentions elsewhere, so I did. I've come to an age where I must consider marriage and children, and if I could not have you, I'd hoped the companionship of someone else might fill the void."

"And? Has it?"

Reaching across the space between them, he cupped her cheek, stroking his thumb along the line of her jaw. "Surely, you must know by now that no one can fill the emptiness that being without you has left in me. One thousand Sybil Beauchamps could not achieve that feat."

Meeting his gaze, she did not speak, but he read doubt in her eyes. Why should she trust him after what he'd done? She might still want him, which was what had brought her to his doorstep tonight, but she did not trust him. Not yet.

"I know you do not believe me," he continued. "I do not expect you to. All I ask is that you allow me to prove to you that I've changed. Let me show you that I am ready to do what I should have done years ago and become your husband. Give me one more chance, and I swear upon pain of death that you will never know hurt by my hand again."

Lowering her eyes, she sighed. "I fear you might be wasting your time, Colin. The truth is, I have no desire to marry anyone."

His fault, that. However, there was no need to say so aloud—they both knew the truth.

Smiling, he shrugged. "Then I won't marry either. As long as you remain unattached, I shall be as well, a tribute to my love for you. If you are not my wife, then I shall take no wife."

"What of Sybil?"

Colin snorted. "She hardly poses a threat to you. Though I find it endearing that you were jealous of her."

She attempted to scowl at him, but failed, laughing instead. Once she had sobered, her expression became solemn once more.

"I don't know what to say. I know that I'm the one who initiated this evening, but I hardly understand why myself. I … I need more time."

He nodded. "I understand. In the interim, I would like to continue spending time with you. Not publicly, of course—Hartford has made it more than clear that I am to maintain my distance. He is watching my every move."

Her eyes widened. "My stepfather spoke with you about me?"

"He warned me against trying to pursue you again. I cannot say I blame the man, either. He loves you as if you were his own flesh and blood, and only thinks to protect you. First, I intend to prove myself to you, then I'll do the same with him. That is … if you'll allow me."

She seemed to think on that for a moment before speaking. "I … I suppose it could not hurt for us to see each other in secret. I cannot deny that I enjoyed what just happened between us. I missed that."

He stroked a lock of her hair, then went back to his brandy. "So did I. The memories of our night at the inn are some of my fondest. They became some of the only things that kept me warm during those lonely nights in Belgium."

Clasping her glass between both hands, she tilted her head and studied him closely. "Was it very awful, Colin? As bad as they say?"

Sighing, he downed what was left of his brandy before crossing the room to pour another measure. Her question had conjured a bitter taste, one he wanted to cleanse his palate of and forget.

"Yes," he stated, without offering any details. She did not need to know the particulars. "But I was one of the few fortunate enough to return home alive. My injury is nothing compared to those that claimed the lives of countless others. I am more privileged than most."

He knew Penelope enough to understand the look on her face. She wished to prod him further, but seemed to think better of it. For that, he was grateful.

After a long pause, she finished her brandy and stood, reaching for her clothing. Downing his second drink in one swallow, he rose to help her fasten her buttons. Placing a kiss on one shoulder, he turned her to face him.

"Allow me to see you home," he said, using his most commanding tone, one that his soldiers had never disobeyed.

While Penelope boasted an independent streak, Colin refused to allow her to walk home alone in the middle of the night. She finished dressing, and waited in silence while he retrieved his coat and hat, then took his offered arm. She held on to it as they navigated the dark lanes back to her address. Content with her company and the cool evening air, he did not strive for conversation. The silence felt comfortable between them, as it always had.

It was not a declaration of love, or a promise of forever. But it was enough to give him hope that eventually, those things would come.

CHAPTER 11

After a yawn-inducing evening of partnering young chits at Almack's—during which he'd been paired with Cassandra twice—Edmond returned home where an empty bed and sleepless night awaited. He felt exhausted from hours of wearing his best false smile while feigning interest in the inane chatter of young girls who had been taught to empty themselves of any and all personality in an effort at nabbing a wealthy husband. Not a single one exhibited the sort of spark that drew him to Penelope. The thought had never been far from his mind all night, thus his melancholy mood. He missed her already, and it had hardly been an entire day since their last encounter.

The reminder that she was not his to want drove him further into the doldrums.

Colin could never know what they'd done, and if it happened again, Edmond must remember it was all he could ever have with her. Besides, he did not have the luxury of pining after a woman uninterested in marriage. There remained his duty to be seen to.

A good night's sleep would make it all seem better by morning, he decided, navigating the front hall to the winding staircase.

The sound of a door opening drew his eye back downstairs. He turned just in time to spy the door to his father's closing on a shadowed figure. Scowling, he stared at the oak panel, wondering who would dare enter the room in the middle of the night. His father would not return home from his evening of gambling until the early hours of the morning. No one ever ventured into the study save the earl, Edmond, the butler, his father's secretary, and the maids who cleaned the room once weekly.

Curious, he descended the way he'd come, ensuring his steps fell silent on the tiled floor. Stepping into the room, he frowned at what he discovered.

A circle of candlelight revealed his mother, her back turned to him. Her graying hair hung down her back in a heavy braid, her short, plump body wrapped in a dressing gown. His father's favorite Agasse painting had been pulled away from the opening it concealed in the wall—where the safe sat, holding important documents and priceless family heirlooms. His jaw fell and he found himself unable to snap his mouth shut at the sight of his mother turning away from the safe, a large cedar box clutched between petite fingers.

She gasped, startled by the sight of him. The cedar box dropped from her grasp and fell to the carpet with a soft thud.

"Edmond," she whispered, guilt making itself evident in her eyes. "I … I was just ..."

"It's all right," he murmured, entering the room and closing the door.

He approached the desk, where her candlestick and taper sat, illuminating her, the Agasse, and the open safe.

"Father is not home. I only came in because I returned a moment ago and heard a noise. I did not realize it was you."

Rounding the desk, he knelt to retrieve her dropped box at the same time she bent and reached for it. Her expression appeared crestfallen when he grasped it first, as if she grew afraid he wouldn't return it to her.

"What do you have here?" he asked, giving her a reassuring smile.

She clenched her hands in front of her, holding fast until her knuckles grew white. Her chin trembled, causing him to frown. Opening the box, he found it filled with trinkets—pieces of jewelry that had likely existed longer than he had. Their rich-hued gems, set in untarnished gold, twinkled in the light of the candle.

He recognized the pieces as those belonging to her before marriage to his father, heirlooms passed down from her great-great-grandmother. The countess only wore the pieces for special occasions, yet Edmond could think of no reason she should need them in the middle of the night.

The realization of what she'd been about caused fury to settle like a stone weight in his gut.

"Mother, what are you doing?"

Lowering her gaze, she sighed. "I only thought ... well, this problem with your father has weighed so heavily on you, Ed. It is not fair. Your father and I brought you into this world, but our problems cannot become your inheritance. Your father's ... weakness ... cannot become your legacy. I had hoped to fetch a good price for these—enough to set our accounts right, perhaps."

Edmond's jaw clenched so hard, his teeth ached as he closed the box. "You will *not* sell your mother's jewels. Or her mother's jewels, or ... well, you get the idea. This predicament is no more your fault than it is mine. I cannot let you sacrifice this part of yourself because of him."

A tear escaped one eye and slid down her wrinkled cheek. "There is nothing left. We have nothing. Your father continues to gamble what little profit we earn from Kesbridge, convinced that all we need is one stroke of good luck to turn our fortune around. I fear he will never stop."

Turning to replace her chest in the safe, he closed it, spinning the lock until it clicked. Once the painting shielded the vault once more, he turned to her again, taking her hands in his.

"Let me worry about him." Releasing one of her hands, he wiped another tear away and forced a smile. "I am your son, and it is my duty to see to you in your old age."

Chuckling, she struck his chest with a playful hand. "Brute. I am hardly an old woman."

He shrugged. "Old enough that you should not live your life in fear of losing everything. You are my mother, and I love you. Let me take care of you. I promise not to let you down."

Her lips quivered when she smiled at him, reaching up to cup his jaw. "You have never let me down, Edmond. You're a good son. I only wish your father and I deserved such a gift."

Leaning down from his considerable height to kiss her cheek, he wrapped his arms around her and held fast—for his own comfort as well as hers.

"Are you mad? The Lord has blessed you with the patience of a saint to have weathered my many mischiefs over the years. Rest easy. I will deal with Father, then expedite my selection of a wife. By Christmas, our accounts will return to good standing, and the coffers of Kesbridge filled. You have my word."

Sniffing, she swiped at her eyes with her hands and nodded. "I apologize for worrying you."

Shaking his head, he offered his arm and took up her candle to escort her back to her room. "Nonsense. There is nothing to apologize for."

Entering the dining room the next morning, Edmond heaved a sigh of resignation. A morning of calls stretched before him, after which he had an engagement to take Miss Cassandra Lane riding in Hyde Park.

His thoughts wandering back to the previous night, he experienced a burst of anger deep in his chest. He hated that his mother had even considered selling her jewels, or that she'd felt the need to secret them from the safe in the dead of night.

No, his mother owed him no apologies. His father, however ... As Edmond entered the dining room, his appetite fled at the sight of the earl seated at the head of the table. Hands curling into fists at his sides, he stomped into the room, casting the butler and footman glares that clearly commanded them to leave. The servants possessed far more respect for him than the earl, and scurried to do his silent bidding. By the time Kesbridge—undoubtedly still a bit foxed from the night before—realized what was happening, the room had cleared.

Grasping the man by his lapels, Edmond heaved him from his seat, propelling him back against the paneled wall, leaving a crack in the wood.

"What the devil?" the earl slurred, his pitiful attempts at dislodging Edmond's hold ineffectual. "Release me this instant!

"Sod off, old man," Edmond muttered, giving him a rough shake.

His actions were rash, but he had decided he could no longer bear this. Besides, his father could not disinherit him, and as the only child, needed him to carry on the family name and lineage. In short, Edmond could act as he bloody well pleased, and there wasn't a damn thing the earl could do about it.

"I am going to talk, and you are going to listen," he continued. "I have had more than enough of your idiocy. You are far too old to behave this way, and it ends now … this minute."

"I haven't the slightest notion what you might mean," the earl blustered, his cheeks reddening as his chest heaved with indignation.

"Do not think to play stupid with me. Your gambling has grown out of hand, and I will no longer stand aside and allow it to continue destroying what is left of *my* inheritance."

The earl raised his chin, leveling a defiant stare at him. "Don't be dramatic. Things aren't nearly so bad as all that. Besides, I won more than I lost last night … my luck's finally turned around. It won't be long yet before—"

"No!" Edmond bellowed. "No more cards, dice, or betting books. No more horse races or cock fights. No more boxing matches! This has nothing to do with luck, and everything to do with chance, which cannot be relied upon. You have harmed this family enough. For

Christ's sake, Mother would have sold her jewels if I hadn't stopped her. All because of you!"

The earl, who loved his wife more than he did gambling, blanched at this news. "She … she what?"

Releasing him, Edmond took a step back, straightening his own rumpled clothes. "I caught her sneaking them from the safe last night. Do you understand, now, the lengths she is willing to go to in order to salvage our good name and your reputation? How dearly she loves you, that she would think to sacrifice something that means so much to save your arse?"

Shuddering, the earl lowered his head. Despite his anger, Edmond pitied his father. The man clearly wrestled with a something far stronger than he.

"There was a time I thought protecting her from the truth to be the most important thing in the world. God help me, Ed, what have I become?" The earl sank to his knees on the floor, leaning back against the wall with a deep sigh. "I cannot stop. The temptation is far too great in London, and the urges … they are unlike anything I've ever known. I realize I sound like a madman, but it is the truth."

Edmond sank down to the floor as well, crossing his legs in front of him as he positioned himself beside his father.

"We all have our vices," he murmured. "For some men, it's drink. Others, laudanum or opium. Myself … well, it's no secret how easily a pair of nice tits can turn my head."

They shared a chuckle over that, as the earl muttered something between chuckles about that being another one of his obsessions.

"You have to try," Edmond stated once they'd quieted. "For Mother, at least, you must try. She has done nothing to deserve this."

Avoiding his gaze out of shame, his father nodded. "You are right, of course. I want to promise you that it will end, but …"

"It will not be easy," he added. "I know. A few mistakes now and then are acceptable. You've got yourself in quite deep."

Running a hand through his thinning hair, the earl pursed his lips, then nodded as if resolved. "There are a few meaningless trinkets and pieces of so-called art in this house that are hardly necessary to our survival. Things none of us will miss. Perhaps their sale can set a few accounts right. After that, your mother and I will quit London before Season's end."

"A wise idea," Edmond agreed. "The country does not offer near as many opportunities to gamble as the city. Perhaps when you return next Season, it will be with a clearer head."

Neither of them spoke of the larger problem at hand. The ancestral seat lay in dire straits, and it would take far more than the sale of a few paintings and snuffboxes to repair it. As much as his parents insisted this could not be his burden to bear, the fact remained that it was—would be until he could secure the mousy yet wealthy Miss Cassandra Lane.

"I never wanted this for you," the earl whispered. "I was fortunate to fall in love with your mother while all my associates found themselves forced into marriages of convenience. I wanted the same for you. For you to be in a position to choose love over duty."

Resting his head against the wall and closing his eyes, he could not chase the image of Penelope from his mind. He'd wanted that for himself as well, yet even if his money woes had not put him in this predicament, his own foolishness would have.

Dash it all, he'd gone and fallen in love with his best friend's woman. The woman his bosom chum wanted to marry. A woman he could never claim in any way but physically. For once in his life, the physical was no longer enough.

CHAPTER 12

*P*enelope took a careful sip of her hot chocolate, sighing as the sweet taste and warmth of it flooded her senses. Comfort in a cup, her mother had always called the drink. Unfortunately, there remained only so much the hot confection could do to soothe her troubles. Having decided a night of respite from the social whirl was in order, she'd dressed for an evening at home—wearing her most comfortable and demure night rail and warmest dressing gown. Curled up in bed with a roaring fire in the hearth, she stared down at the pages of a book she could hardly remember a word of.

She'd been looking forward to finding time to read her copy of *Glenarvon*, the scandalous, anonymously published novel that had the *ton* in an uproar. Despite the supposed outrage of many of the *ton*'s most distinguished members, the book's shocking content had become the topic of conversation in every drawing room, ballroom, and gentleman's club in the city.

Yet, now that she had discreetly acquired a copy, she could not muster an ounce of interest in the sensational events of Calantha's life. Rather, she found herself focused on the melodrama of her own making.

She'd thought that engaging in love affairs with both Colin and Edmond would satisfy her—sating her physical desires, while repaying them both for their duplicity. Yet, all it had done was muddle her head.

First, there had been Edmond, who had surprised her with his dominant hand in the bedroom—or, carriage. She'd set out to seduce him, but had found herself overcome, unsure by the end which of them had actually held the upper hand. However, it had been his tenderness afterward that had disarmed her, remaining with her long after the physical euphoria had faded.

And Colin ... her chest ached as she remembered his impassioned words.

"Give me one more chance, and I swear upon pain of death that you will never know hurt by my hand again."

Yet, the revelation that he would conspire with Edmond to trick her had hurt. Once had not been enough, when he could so easily make a fool of her. After all, she had, indeed, become jealous of Sybil Beauchamp, just as he'd intended. Yet, the sincerity in his gaze as he'd promised to prove his love to her gave her pause. Could he have been telling the truth all along? Did he really love her?

"No," she murmured to herself. "It's all a farce ... just a game men play."

It was true, and Penelope had seen it happen countless times. She had allowed a man to play with her heart once—she would not allow it to happen again. Let Colin think she was softening toward him! Let Edmond believe she was finished with his best friend and wanted only him! Let them both drive themselves mad trying to win her ... in the end, she would belong to no one but herself.

Closing her eyes, she allowed her mind to wander back to her encounter with Colin the night before. Her cheeks warmed at the memory, and the surface of her skin began to tingle. While it had not lasted very long, every second of it had proven to be pure rapture, and she found herself longing for more. Or perhaps, it was more of Edmond's domination she needed. Sighing, she forgot her book and allowed her mind to wander. She imagined Edmond here with her now, undressing her and stretching her body across the bed. Biting her lower lip, she envisioned the soft fabric of his cravat binding her wrists to the bedpost. His leafy green eyes would gleam like dark emeralds as he lay between her legs, fucking her with hard and fast strokes.

Yet, all of a sudden, Colin's face appeared within her field of vision, despite Edmond's presence between her thighs. His face filled with naked lust for her, he knelt beside her, hands kneading her breasts in a steady rhythm, his fingers on her nipples heightening the pleasure of Edmond's strokes.

Moaning, she lifted her nightgown, finding the curls blanketing her mons wet from desire. Just the thought of the two men touching her, one suckling her breast while the other fucked her, made her tremble.

As her fingers encountered the slick flesh, she allowed her fantasy full rein, picturing every wicked thing she could conjure. She bit back a cry as her insides quivered, her mind running wild with fancies of Colin filling her mouth and thrusting with wild abandon while Edmond knelt behind her, pounding into her without restraint, all while her hands remained tied, leaving her at their mercy.

She splintered with a whimper, her core clenching around her fingers as she plunged them deep, heightening her pleasure. Fighting to control her harsh breathing, Penelope kept her eyes closed, not ready to relinquish her daydream just yet. It seemed far preferable to pondering emotions she did not wish to feel.

The following morning, she found the marquis awaiting her in the dining room—a rare occurrence. He typically opted to have tea and toast at his desk in the mornings, preferring to attend his business as early as possible, before schmoozing other politicians over lunch at one of his clubs and attending sessions at the House of Lords.

Giving him a bright smile, she took her seat at his left, waiting for her tea and biscuits to appear before her.

"Good morning," she chirped, injecting her tone with cheer.

The last thing she needed was for him to detect her state of exhaustion due to a sleepless night. Tossing and turning in bed, she'd been unable to turn her thoughts from either Colin or Edmond. Thinking of one inevitably led to contemplating the other, until she found her thoughts overcome by them.

"Good morning, dearest," he mumbled, his eyelids lowered as he perused his crisp, ironed copy of the *London Gazette*.

The servant appeared with her breakfast, and she stirred sugar and milk into her tea and slathered her biscuits with butter and jam. Hartford's gaze raised to her and held—probing, steady.

"Did you enjoy your quiet evening at home?" he inquired between sips of his own tea.

She nodded, chewing a bite of biscuit and swallowing before answering him. "Oh, yes. It was quite lovely. I enjoy London, but the constant social whirl can grow exhausting at times."

Lifting his eyebrows, he gave her a pointed look. "Yet, you plan to reside here permanently once you come of age."

Her spine straightened at his words, knowing all-too well what would come next. It was a conversation they'd had several times, and it should come as no surprise he would broach the subject with her given her twenty-fifth birthday now looming less than a month away.

"I see no reason to follow you and Mother back and forth every Season once I become the proud owner of my own townhouse and have hired a suitable companion. Besides, everything I could ever need is here. In your old age, you and Mother are entitled to enjoy your time together without me underfoot all the time."

He smiled, the lines around his eyes becoming more prominent. "We love having you around, dearest."

She returned his smile. "I am not a girl anymore, Papa. It is time I make my own way in the world. You needn't worry—I shall be quite all right."

He nodded, leaning back in his high-backed chair. "Of course you shall. Yet, it is difficult for me not to worry, you know. A father needs to know his daughter will be safe and protected. It is difficult for me not to worry that you might have been too rash in your decision regarding marriage."

Her fingers tightened around the handle of her teacup, and she drew in a shaky breath. "Well, I do not. I meant it then, just as I mean it now. Marriage is out of the question. There is not a single man in London I wish to bind myself to for the rest of my life."

Pursing his lips, the marquis inclined his head. "Not even Lord Edmond Ingham?"

The blood in her veins ran cold at his question. Did he *know?*

Tamping down the panic rising in her chest, she took another sip of tea and reminded herself he couldn't possibly. He simply asked because he must have noticed them spending a great deal of time together. First their dance at the Avonleah ball, then a walk the following day, and the picnic later that week, followed by their night at the theater. The marquis proved astute to have noticed something … even if he did not know the full extent of it.

"Don't be silly," she scoffed, waving a dismissive hand. "Edmond is only a dear friend. Besides, I have it on good authority that he's set his sights on Miss Cassandra Lane."

Hartford scowled. "Miss Lane? That whey-faced chit isn't half as beautiful as you."

She laughed. "Perhaps not, but I am on the shelf—a fact that has become common knowledge."

"Do not pretend to be ignorant of the fact that every eligible bachelor in London would come knocking on this door if they thought there existed even the slightest chance—"

"But there isn't one," she insisted, her tone becoming sharper. "Papa, I know you mean well, but please … let it be. I am happy the way things are."

Reaching for her hand, he gave it a squeeze. "Of course, forgive me."

As they finished their meal, she found it hard to forget. She'd lied by telling him she was happy. In truth, she hadn't been happy since the morning she'd awakened to find Colin gone with his letter folded on the pillow beside her. However, she'd vowed to make her own joy. Unlike many other ladies of her acquaintance, she had not allowed herself to believe she needed a man to be content. All men had ever done was seek to use her. Well, she had turned the tables on them, and did not intend to stop now. By Season's end, she would have gotten her revenge on both, and would walk away without an ounce of regret.

If anything, the only thing she might mourn was that she'd never know what it was like to have them both at the same time. Thinking of her imaginations from the night before—of being shared by Edmond and Colin, filled by both of them at once—she shivered.

CHAPTER 13

Colin watched Edmond from across the table they shared at White's, curiosity furrowing his brow. While he had awakened in a chipper mood and carried the feeling with him everywhere he went, Edmond's disposition had become positively dismal. It was if they'd traded places—Colin stepping beneath the umbrella of his best friend's typically sunny demeanor, while Edmond had taken residence beneath Colin's raincloud of misery.

Even the pain throbbing from his hip to his thigh could not rob him of the smile he'd been wearing since leaving Penelope at the back gate leading into the garden of her family's townhouse. He'd left her there with a kiss, watching until she'd disappeared into the house, then taken his time walking home, enjoying the crisp night air.

His men had teased him mercilessly about his lack of desire for whores and camp followers during the war. Month after month, year after year, he had gone without sexual release, saving himself for the only woman he wanted in his bed until the day he died. The night she had come to him had proved the fulfillment of every dream he'd indulged in during those cold, sleepless nights—times he'd wondered if he would even make it back to her alive.

"Are you quite certain you're all right?" Colin asked, watching his friend's face for any sign of the reason for his dark mood. "You've been in a dudgeon all day."

Pursing his lip, Edmond lowered his bloodshot eyes to the tumbler of port held between his hands. "Nothing new … the usual."

Ah. His father must have been at it again. He knew the burden of Edmond's family's problem weighed heavily on him; yet, he couldn't put off the nagging suspicion there might be more to it than that. However, he did not want to pry. One thing he had come to learn about Edmond was that he would speak on the matter in his own time. When he wanted Colin to know, he would tell him everything.

"I'm sorry," he murmured. "I should not have asked."

Edmond shrugged. "It's not as if any of it is your fault."

"No, but it isn't yours, either. Don't be so hard on yourself, Ed." After a moment of silence, he perked up and smiled. "I know! How about a few hours pommeling the coxcombs at Gentleman Jacks? A few rounds in the ring always makes you feel better."

He scowled. "I can't. I have an engagement to go riding with Miss Lane."

So that was the other piece of the puzzle. Edmond had selected his wealthy heiress and had begun the pursuit. He must feel like a man headed to the hangman's noose. Very soon, his fate would become unavoidable. The notion made Colin feel a bit guilty for being so bloody happy about Penelope.

"I see. How about this evening? Dinner and cards at Watier's? Dinner on my account."

Sighing, Edmond continued avoiding his gaze, draining what remained of his port and pushing his untouched lunch plate aside.

"Sorry, old chap. I'm not feeling at all the thing today. I'm afraid I'll have to cry off. After my ride with Miss Lane, I intend to retire early. Perhaps another time."

Standing, Edmond gave him an apologetic glance before disappearing, his long limbs carrying him across the room so swiftly, Colin could never hope to catch him up with his leg in such a state.

Remaining in his seat, he took up his own port and took a slow sip, ruminating over the strange conversation. Edmond had been behaving so bloody strangely these days, but Colin understood his friend had his own problems. It became difficult not to take his slights personally, yet he knew it had nothing to do with him. Edmond simply needed space, he supposed.

Besides, the refusal of his invitation left him free to attempt to see Penelope. With a grin, he contemplated climbing the ivy-covered trellis to her window, slipping inside, and awakening her with a kiss. It was something he'd done when first falling in love with her, unable to go even one day without tasting her lips. Their innocent touches and caresses had set her cheeks aflame with pink blossoms—her being a maiden and all. Now, he wouldn't stop at simply touching and tasting. He would claim her as he had the night she'd come to him. He'd return every night if he had to, never letting her forget how badly he needed her.

Realizing he grew aroused just thinking about it, he forced his thoughts to shift, hoping to focus his attention elsewhere. When he glanced up, he found a familiar gentleman walking toward him through the crowded club. Snapping to attention, he stood, saluting Major-General Sir Henry Torrens, the Military Secretary of London's War Office.

"Major," he said.

"Captain Worthing," Torrens murmured, returning the salute. "Just the man I've come to see."

Colin could not hide his surprise at the major-general's words. "Me, Sir?"

Torrens chuckled. "Yes, you. Are you here with someone, or might I have a moment of your time?"

"My companion just left," he replied, gesturing toward Edmond's empty chair. "Please, join me."

As the major-general took the offered seat, Colin hailed a waiter, who appeared to take Edmond's abandoned plate and glass. He returned with more port and a clean tumbler before leaving them again.

Colin couldn't help a feeling of dread over the reason for this meeting. Torrens' department was responsible for overseeing army personnel.

Had he come under disciplinary action for some reason?

"I'd intended to have you summoned to the War Office," Torrens declared. "However, once I learned that you frequented this club, I thought a more informal meeting might be in order."

Then he wasn't in trouble. That relieved him only slightly.

"Of course," he replied, trying to remain patient. "What may I do for you, Sir?"

"I'll come right to the point, Captain," Torrens declared. "With the war behind us, the time has come for many of England's men-at-arms to contemplate their futures. While peace is a victory hard fought and won, the fact remains that it means far too few opportunities for the men who fought the battles. A man cannot live on half-pay alone."

Colin knew this well enough. If it weren't for his monthly allowance, his army half-pay would not prove nearly enough to cover his living expenses. Many of his men had been forced to seek other means of securing income after Waterloo, as most did not hail from the upper class as he did.

"I am a fortunate man," he replied, uncertain of what else to say. "My family estates and good name see me well taken care of. I am happy to live on half-pay until such time as I am needed again."

"You are needed now," Torrens stated.

Panic gripped him, robbing him of air at the prospect of a new conflict. The metallic taste of blood suddenly filled his mouth, and he realized he'd bit down on the inside of his cheek when clenching his teeth. The pain in his thigh seemed to increase, reminding him of the bayonet that had caused it. Even with his eyes open, he could see the French soldier in his blue coat, a vicious snarl curling his lips as he thrust the bayonet toward him with vicious intent.

"What has happened?" he asked, afraid to hear the answer. He was no coward, but he had hardly healed from the last battle—barely escaping with his life.

"Nothing that should put that shade of green in your face, young man," the major-general said in a soothing tone, seeming to sense Colin's distress. "Calm yourself."

Taking a drink with a shaking hand, he nodded. "I'm all right."

"I'm here to offer you a position ... working for me at the War Office."

Colin's eyebrows shot up as he lifted his gaze to meet that of his superior. Annoyance suddenly gripped him, as he realized what was happening.

"I might have guessed you would try this," he said, fighting to keep his voice even. "I refused your offer of monetary reward upon your return to London, remember?"

"This is not about that," Torrens retorted, lowering his voice. "I accept that you wish to be modest about your heroism—"

"I did my duty," Colin interjected. "Nothing more."

"You saved my life," the major-general insisted. "And the lives of many others. If you had not gathered those men after your captain turned craven, things might not have happened the way they did."

"Of course they wouldn't have," Colin retorted. "The men who were foolish enough to follow me might still be alive."

Torrens grimaced. "There are many things I'm certain we both wish could have been different, Captain. Yet, you know as well as I do that it isn't possible. So we must move forward."

"A battlefield promotion was far more than I deserved, and I had no choice but to accept it. When Wellington gives a gift ..."

The major-general chuckled. "You certainly couldn't have turned him down as easily as you have done me. Listen ... this offer has nothing to do with me wanting to repay you for saving my life. I am offering you the position because I trust you, and you deserve it. Your decision to purchase a commission seemed rash at the time, but you've more than proven yourself a capable soldier and a good man."

Producing a thick envelope from the inside pocket of his coat, Torrens slid it across the table, placing it in front of him.

"Inside are the details of the position. Take as much time as you need to read it over and make a decision. I am not considering anyone else unless you turn me down. Think of your future, Captain. You are of an age where marriage is inevitable, as are children. What sort of legacy will you leave them? Will you support them on army half-pay and scraps from your brother's table your entire life?"

Without waiting for an answer, Torrens stood, finishing his port.

"You may send word to War Office once you've reached a decision," he added. "Or, simply present yourself. I hope you will make the right decision."

Leaving him alone once more, the major-general disappeared into the crowded club, greeting acquaintances as he made his way toward the door.

Staring down at the envelope, Colin was left with no choice but to take it up, stuffing it into the pocket of his own coat.

Forgetting the events of Waterloo leading up to his injury and the death of almost his entire regiment had been his sole aim, aside from healing and winning Penelope back. Now, the man whose life he had saved at the expense of several others wished to continue reminding him. How could he be expected to face the man day after day, constantly reminded of a time he wished he could banish from his memory completely?

Nonetheless, the major-general's words lingered. Having to live on his father and brother's mercy had always chafed. More so now that he had become a new man. A man who had been to war, and killed. A man who had led and commanded, even when those he was supposed to follow had failed him.

What did he have to offer Penelope other than his name and his love? At one time, it might have been enough. Now, she had nearly reached her majority and that would make her wealthier than he could ever hope to be as a third son on half-pay from the army. While he knew it never would have mattered to her, he still felt a sense of obligation to provide. Aside from that, he *wanted* to do it, to perhaps earn her pride in him that he had made something of himself.

Leaving the club, he leaned heavily on his walking stick, the pain in his thigh reaching near unbearable limits. During the entire walk home, he remained ever-aware of the heavy envelope against his chest.

CHAPTER 14

$\mathcal{E}$dmond paced the length of the garden, hands clenched tight behind his back. The hour had passed two o'clock in the morning ten minutes ago, and Penelope was late. She had responded to his message, sent by his valet—the only man he trusted with such a sensitive note. Soon after, her abigail had slipped an answer into his man's hand: her acceptance of his request that she come to him tonight at two of the clock. While he had wanted to come for her himself, he remained aware that it wouldn't be wise. Besides, he was not oblivious to her experience in discreet affairs. She knew how to go unseen in the dark of night, and he felt confident she would arrive unharmed.

The longer she kept him waiting, the more anxious he became, imagining some harsh fate befalling her with him powerless to stop it.

It would be your own fault, he told himself. *Just as this entire debacle has been.*

Yes, it was his fault, all of it. When Colin had asked him to speak with Penelope on his behalf, he should have refused. Or, when he'd danced with her that night, he should not have engaged her in flirting, a habit he found himself slipping into far too easily. He should never have kissed her that first time in the alley, or fucked her in his carriage. He should never have allowed himself to even think of her as anything other than Colin's future bride.

Now, he found himself waiting in a dark garden for a woman he wasn't supposed to desire, but could not stop thinking about, while a confused mixture of guilt and anticipation swirled low in his gut.

The sound of horse's hooves mingled with the clatter of carriage wheels disturbed his thoughts, bringing him to his feet. Walking to the garden gate, he peered over it into the darkness, waiting to determine if what he'd heard had been her arrival. A sigh of relief rushed between his lips when a slight figure shrouded in a dark, hooded cloak appeared from the alley, walking toward him at a brisk pace.

Not bothering to unlatch the gate, he vaulted over it, rushing forward to meet her at a jog. As he drew near, she lowered the hood of her cloak, allowing the moonlight to illuminate her face. She smiled when he reached for her, slipping one hand into the folds of her cloak to grasp her waist. The other cupped her face, tilting her head back for a kiss.

She melted against him as he took her mouth, his lips possessing her with a tenderness that surprised even him. Sinking against her body, he cradled her soft curves with his hard planes, reveling in the moment. They weren't in a carriage, hurrying to finish before arriving at her home. No one was coming who might see them kissing out in the open.

When he pulled away, her eyes had grown heavy-lidded, and her breath raced between parted lips turned red and swollen from his kisses.

"Well," she murmured, clearly stunned by his tender assault. "Good evening to you, too."

"I've missed you," he replied, taking her hand to lead her back toward the garden.

"I missed you, as well," she said, allowing him to open the gate before preceding him through it.

Taking her hand again, he pulled her through to one of the

servants' entrances, which led them along a long, dark corridor. They traversed it in silence, then scaled several flights of rough, wooden stairs before Edmond found the correct door. They appeared in his dressing room, which he promptly led her through to his bedchamber.

Sweeping into the space as if she owned it, Penelope removed her cloak, draping it over the back of an armchair near the fire.

"What's all this?" she asked, gesturing toward the spread he had arranged on a blanket before the fire in order to pass the time.

Removing his own coat, he tossed it on top of her cloak and reached for her once more, taking her into his arms and holding her close.

"I did not only ask you here to fuck, Penelope. I truly did miss your company these last few days. I thought we could talk first. Have some wine. Spend time together."

Her eyes widened, and something akin to fear seemed to alight in her gaze.

Are you frightened, sweet Penny? I am, as well.

She smiled again, yet this time, it seemed forced. "You didn't have to go through so much trouble for me, Edmond. I've never required romance of my past lovers."

Lifting one of her hands, he lightly kissed the knuckles. "You shall have it with me. Now, sit, please. Let me pour you a glass of wine."

He released her, watching as she sank to her knees on the floor, arranging her skirts decorously about her legs. He joined her, plucking the bottle of champagne he had procured for them from its ice bucket, and filling two flutes. After handing her one, he raised his glass to her before taking a drink. She followed suit, draining about half the contents before reaching out to pluck a plump grape from the platter he had arranged them on.

"How was your day?" she asked, reaching for another grape.

Sighing, he stretched out until he lay on his side, staring up at her. "Hellish. I do not wish to speak of it, not while you're here. I asked you here because I knew you could help me forget."

Reaching out, she smoothed her soft fingers over his furrowed brow, soothing the lines. Stroking his hair back from his face, she frowned.

"My dear Edmond ... I do not like seeing you this way. What can I do?"

"Your presence is enough," he replied, placing his glass aside and lying down to rest his head in her lap. "You have the strange ability to brighten a man's world, Penelope. When you are with me, I forget everything except you."

She stiffened, her fingers pausing on their journey through his hair. He closed his eyes, realizing now that he had gone too far. Penelope was a pragmatic woman, one who did not make room for attachments in her life. However, he had become far too captivated by her, far too quickly. How pitiful she must think him.

"Shall I tell you about my day, then?"

Grateful for a change of subject, he nodded, turning onto his back so he could look up at her. "Yes, please."

She finished her first glass of champagne, then reached out for the bottle, refilling her flute. "Well, after morning calls, I spent my afternoon inspecting townhouses for sale."

That caught his attention. He realized her twenty-fifth birthday loomed near, and with its coming, her inheritance and independence would both become hers.

"That sounds exciting," he said, for lack of anything better to say.

What else could he say?

Well, darling, that sounds marvelous, but you and I both know you'll never purchase a home on your own before Colin has swooped in to claim you.

The thought of them, perhaps purchasing a home together instead caused a heavy, cold weight to settle in his gut.

"Oh, it was," she said with a nod. "I believe I've found the one, too. A lovely home on Half Moon Street, with wrought iron railings on the stairs, and beautiful marble floors. Grecian columns in the front hall, four drawing rooms, a music room, and a sunroom, as well. It is perfect."

"What will you do in such a house by yourself?" he asked, genuinely interested to hear her answer.

She shrugged, then giggled. "Entertain, I suppose. Enjoy my solitude. Whatever I bloody want, that's for certain. Nothing will feel better than owning myself, as well as my own home, outright."

Falling silent, he thought over her words for a moment. If she held true to her word, the next year and the one after would see her firmly on the shelf. It was the life she claimed to want, but Edmond could not help but wonder ... somewhere inside her, the girl who had loved Colin Worthing enough to risk scandal for a marriage that never happened must still reside.

"That sort of life may suit you for a time," he mused aloud. "But one year from now? Five years? Won't you become lonely in such an existence?"

She scoffed. "Only a man who believes a woman's sole option in this world is to marry a man and birth his children would ask such a question."

Edmond laughed. "That might be true, but that does not only apply to women, you know. A man like me has only one option, as well, and it isn't much different. For me, marriage is a must, as well as the siring of an heir. The difference is, I am also expected to inherit my father's title, lands, and reputation. I could not choose an alternate future, even if I wanted to."

She gazed own at him for a moment in silence, her expression pensive. "I never thought of it that way. Men of the upper class seem the most privileged in our world. I never stopped to think that first sons are as much slaves to society's expectations as we are."

Chuckling again, he reached up and tugged a loose lock of her hair. "Well, I *am* allowed to vote. That, and the benefits of other privileges you don't have isn't lost on me, darling. I did not mean to imply that my plight is so difficult as that of a woman. I just thought ... well, I imagine a different sort of life for you."

She scoffed. "Pray, do tell, Edmond."

"Well," he began. "I imagine you being awakened every morning by a husband who is madly in love with you. As the sun rises through the window, casting its rays on your hair, just so ... he finds himself overcome by your beauty. So much so that he must have you then and there. You begin most of your mornings that way, I think."

With a laugh, she shifted until she rested on her hip, legs folded beside her. His head remained in her lap.

"I like it already," she murmured.

"After breakfast, you adjourn to the schoolroom to look in on your two children. As you watch them at their lessons with the governess, your heart swells with pride, and you press a hand to your round, swollen belly, thinking of the one soon to join his elder brother and sister."

Snorting, she nearly choked on the grape she nibbled. "*Three* children in five years?"

Edmond shrugged. "You are fertile, and your husband is virile. However, being a wife and mother aren't the only things you excel at. After meeting with your housekeeper to go over the decadent menu for your dinner party later that evening, you depart for an afternoon of work with your charitable ladies' society ... a new group of upper class wives you assembled yourself for the impact of maximum influence through their husbands. Everyone thinks all you do is sew stockings and pass packets of medicine out to the poor. Ah, but your true aim is to exert influence upon your husbands, swaying their positions and votes in the House of Lords. As a group, you get them to do your bidding by withholding intercourse and their favorite brandy, you wily minxes!"

Fits of laughter shook her, until she collapsed almost on top of him. "What a ridiculous notion, that men can be so easily manipulated by their wives!"

Edmond arched an eyebrow at her. "You know appallingly little about men if you find that notion ridiculous. Besides, I've heard of such tactics being quite successful. Nonetheless ... back to your life. It would be a full one, Penelope … a busy existence, but one filled with people and love."

"And my husband allows me freedom of movement?" she asked, a hint of sarcasm in her voice. "I think not."

Rising to a seated position, he reached up and cupped her face. "Darling, your husband is so batty for you, he'd move a mountain if you asked it. He allows your every whim and fulfills your every desire, because his existence is reduced to nothing if you aren't happy."

Despite the desire flaming in her gaze, she frowned, the expression at odds with what he found in her eyes, and he suspected, what she found in her own heart.

"You are referring to Colin, aren't you?" she murmured.

Clenching his jaw, he realized she was right. He *had* thought of her with Colin, because he hadn't allowed himself to imagine things any other way. Yet now, with her lying in his arms, capturing him with her wide-eyed stare, he allowed himself to believe otherwise—that, perhaps, there might be a chance she could be his.

"No," he replied, his voice low and raspy to his own ears. "I am not referring to Colin."

He slid his hand back to grasp the nape of her neck, commanding her without words to come to him. Her hesitation didn't last long. His flexing fingers massaging her neck stole her resistance, and she met his lips with a breathy sigh.

His kiss became urgent his time, lacking his earlier warmth and finesse. He hungered for her, lapping at her with his tongue, yearning for her taste. They moaned in unison, desire crackling in the air between them like lightning.

"Shall I show you how the Penelope of my dreams spends her nights?" he whispered.

Before she could answer, he was standing, taking her up into his arms. Cradled against his chest, she held on to his neck, resting her head against his shoulder. Once they reached the massive bed taking up an entire corner of the chamber, he laid her down upon her stomach. He removed his cravat, waistcoat, and shirt before climbing onto the bed, straddling her hips and leaning down to press his naked chest against her back.

Pushing a lock of hair aside, he kissed her jaw, then moved down to the sensual curve of her neck. She sighed when he kissed her there, tracing a path to her shoulder. As he continued on his way, Edmond brought his fingers to the fastenings of her gown, swiftly opening them. His mouth followed his hands, the satin ribbons of her corset tickling his lips. When he reached the ribbon at her tailbone, he caught it between his teeth and tugged, loosening the neat bow her abigail had accomplished. He loosened the confining garment, then pulled it, along with her gown and chemise, away from her body at once, lifting her to gingerly peel the layers away. Standing, he tossed the clothing into a heap on the floor before removing her dainty slippers, throwing them aside, as well.

"Christ, I wish you could see what a pretty picture you make," he murmured, reaching down to apply pressure to his aching cock. "Your long legs in those silk stockings, the rest of your body bare just for me. Your lovely back, the perfect curve of your luscious arse. Part your legs for me, darling."

Arching her back and bending her knees, she lifted her hips from the bed and exposed the tender pink flesh of her quim. He approached the bed, reaching out to palm one of the soft cheeks of her derrière. He smoothed his hand over it, tracing the curve up to her back, then down, skimming her spine with his fingers. Following the same path, he moved back down, smoothing the pad of his index finger along each bump of her spine, then delving between her cheeks. Pressing his thumb against the tight opening of her rear passage, he smiled when she shuddered.

"Do you like that, love? It's all right for you to talk this time ... I haven't produced the gag ... yet."

She shivered again, as if the prospect of him gagging her again excited her. "Yes," she whispered. "Yes, I liked it."

He nodded, circling the bed until he stood before her. "Good."

Reaching out for the tassel holding the bed curtains tethered to the post, he untied it, then grasped one of her hands. She fell forward onto her stomach when he grasped the other, throwing her off balance. He executed a quick, efficient knot, trapping her wrists together before lifting them and securing them both to the post. Testing his handiwork, he determined that he hadn't tied her too tight.

Grasping the ropes with both hands, she used the leverage of the post to rise to her knees, facing him.

Reaching out to pinch one of her nipples, he smiled when she whimpered. He palmed one heavy breast, watching as the tip went hard against his hand. He took the other in hand, as well, kneading them both before caressing the nipples lightly with his thumbs. Bending his head, he dragged his tongue over first one, then the other.

Grasping the ropes, she held on tight, moaning as he took one deep into his mouth and suckled with powerful tugs while steadily teasing the nipple with his tongue.

Releasing her, he circled the bed again, climbing up behind her. While unfastening his breeches with one hand, he slid the other between her open legs, encountering the slick, wet folds of her cunt. She moaned, wiggling her hips and angling herself closer to him. He slid two fingers inside of her, trembling as he found her dripping wet for him.

Stroking her velvety channel, he placed his thumb against her anus once more, pressing with gentle insistence. She drew a sharp breath, raised her hips, and invited him in. Encouraged by her response, he withdrew his fingers from her cunt, using them to smear her in her own wetness. When she was ready, he replaced his fingers inside her, then returned his thumb to her now readied rear opening. It slid inside her with ease, and the tight ring of flesh gripped him.

"Ah, Edmond, yes!" she cried, her breath coming in harsh gasps as he slowly plunged and withdrew all three digits, invading both spaces simultaneously, stroking her to greater heights of pleasure.

He licked his lips, his fascinated gaze locked on the sight of his thumb disappearing into that secret part of her … a part he longed to explore further.

"You're such a naughty girl, Penelope," he groaned, removing his fingers from her sheath, but keeping his thumb buried deep. "I should punish you for being so wicked."

A throaty laugh escaped her lips, followed by a moan as he pressed the swollen head of his sex against her opening.

"Yes, punish me, Edmond," she gasped as he teased her dewy folds and the button of her clit, rubbing his cock back and forth against her.

Grasping a handful of her hair, he gave it a tug, pulling her head back until his mouth could reach her ear. He bit her earlobe, then soothed it with his tongue. Withdrawing his thumb from her, he swiftly slapped her bottom while thrusting into her cunt in one smooth stroke. She screamed, arching her back as her channel began to spasm around him in climax. Holding her hair in one hand, he began to fuck her, pounding against her without restraint. She grasped the bedpost as he pressed her against it, his wild thrusts causing the bed to tremble and shake. Her untamed cries echoed from his high ceilings.

"God damn it, you feel so bloody good. Christ, Penelope!"

She whimpered at the sound of her name shouted in passion, undulating her hips to meet his movements. Turning her head, she met his searching lips, accepting the invasion of his tongue and meeting it with her own.

A moment later, she shuddered again, falling back against him with a weakly muttered, "Edmond".

When she collapsed in his arms, he reached out to untie her, freeing her wrists with a few swift tugs. Turning to lay her against the pillows, he came down between her legs, entering her once more.

Grasping her hands, he pressed them to the bed, intertwining her fingers with his. He slowed his thrusts, closing his eyes as the urge to savor every second suddenly overcame him. His heart pounded in his chest, his every sense heightened as if attuned to hers. Never had he felt so consumed by a woman while taking her to bed. He did not want it to end … not when she held on to his hands as if for dear life, raising her head to capture his mouth in a sweet kiss.

"My darling Penelope," he murmured against her lips. "What have you done to me? I am ruined."

Her wide eyes met his, and he saw and felt her fear as surely as he experienced his own. Yet, he couldn't stop, not when it seemed as if the euphoria of baring his soul while being inside of her might kill him.

"I love you," he groaned as climax began to bear down on him. "I know I shouldn't, but I can't stop … I love you."

He slowed his strokes, hoping to draw it out a moment longer, but when she cried out one last time, her sheath tightening around him in yet another sweet ending, he could stand it no longer. Withdrawing, he spilled on the sheets with a hoarse shout, trembling as the force of his completion stole his breath. All of his anger, sadness, and need trickled from him in a hot rush, until he felt purged … sated.

For a moment, he simply remained where he was, knelt between Penelope's spread knees, head lowered. He feared what he might see if he looked at her, yet knew he could not avoid the inevitable any longer. When he lifted his gaze, his gut roiled at what he found.

Breath coming in short, ragged gasps, she glared at him, tears spilling over the rims of her eyes. While he had not expected her to respond with a similar declaration of her own, he certainly hadn't expected this.

"Get up," she growled from between clenched teeth. "Remove yourself from my person this instant."

Bewildered, he obeyed, standing to reach for his breeches. Fumbling with shaking hands, she tore her chemise free from the clothing he'd left in a heap on the floor. Frowning, he watched as she snatched it on, all while avoiding his gaze.

"Penelope, please talk to me. What did I do? Was I too rough? I didn't hurt you, did I?"

The notion horrified him, so he quickly closed the distance between them, reaching out to clutch her shoulders.

"Look at me ... please."

When she did, her gaze might have killed him if it were capable. She glared at him as if he were the vilest snake to be crushed beneath her boot. Before he could register her intent, her palm made contact with his cheek with a surprising amount of strength. The sting of it spread from his cheek to his jaw and up toward his eye, causing it to water.

"You son of a bitch," she murmured. "You lecher."

Grasping his face, he stared at her with wide eyes. "What the bloody hell was that all about?"

"How dare you speak to me of love when you've been lying to me this entire time?"

The niggling sensation of dread prickled along the surface of his skin. "What are you talking about?"

"Don't play stupid, Edmond," she spat. "Did you, or did you not, agree to help Colin manipulate me into marriage with him?"

Her question slammed into him, knocking the air from his lungs. "I ... well, I ... it isn't so simple as all that."

She slapped him again, harder this time.

"Ah, bloody hell!" he muttered, left with no choice but to accept what was happening.

After all, she was right. He *had* agreed, then he had allowed himself to cross the line with her, in more ways than one.

"All right," he relented. "I did ... he asked for my help and I agreed."

"How could you?" she demanded, another tear racing down one cheek. "After all he did to me, you—you conspired with him ... and for what? Did it amuse you both to toy with me? Or does he not know that you made sport of me, pursuing me even after agreeing to help steer me in his direction? I'm certain it was so much fun for you, Edmond, helping yourself to Colin's leavings."

"Now wait just one moment," he protested, a sudden thought occurred to him. "I might have agreed to help Colin, but *you* practically threw yourself at me in that carriage!"

She laughed, the sound harsh. "Yes, because I knew what you

wanted. Men are so predictable, and you took the bait just as I knew you would."

His mouth fell open until he felt as if his jaw might scrape the floor. "You knew about Colin before you offered yourself to me. Why? Why would you do something like that?"

A sneer marred her beautiful mouth and she crossed her arms over her chest. "Would you ask that question if I were a man? Of course not! Because you do as you please, the lot of you. Well, I'll tell you why. I wanted you both to know how it feels to be toyed with, for once, to lose the upper hand to someone who is keen to your game. Oh, I don't blame you entirely. Colin is just as guilty … but you … I cannot believe you think I can be so easily manipulated with words of love and stories about dreams of the future."

And that's when Edmond understood. Her anger with him did not lie in his pact with Colin. He had dared to bring softer feelings into an affair that was supposed to have been about the physical act, and perhaps revenge, as well. He'd ruined everything by daring to love her.

"You're right," he said. "I am a liar and a cad. Not only am I the worst friend in all of Christendom, I am also a fool. I'm a fool because I thought having your body would be enough, that no one ever had to know, and that once I had purged myself of my desires, we could both be on our way … you wed to Colin, me married to whichever rich chit decides to accept my offer. But I'm such a fool, Penelope, because I let myself fall in love with you."

Shaking her head, she tore her gaze from him and fixed it on some point over his shoulder.

"Stop," she whispered as if pained. "Stop lying to me. I'm sick to death of you men and your lies."

"Say what you will, but I am not lying. The problem is, you know I am not, and if you were willing to be honest with yourself for one moment, I believe you would realize it's the truth and that is why you're angry. Because this was about vengeance for you, but it became about something else. I love you, and you can pretend you don't care about me until the end of time, but I know the truth. You feel something for me; I know you do. Why else would you be crying at the thought that I might care about you, too?"

For a long while, she said nothing. Edmond stood, staring at her profile, watching as the dam holding her emotions in check began to crumble. Never had he wanted to hold her more, to kiss her and lavish her with affection. Damn Colin—the bastard really had ruined her ... but not in the way he thought. Penelope had become bitter and jaded, and Edmond could not blame her.

Eventually, she moved, reaching for her corset. Turning away from him, she slipped it on and began tightening the ribbons herself.

"Get me a hansom cab," she said, her voice hoarse from crying. "I am going home. You are never to speak to me again."

Left with no other recourse, Edmond could do nothing but obey. Reaching for his shirt, he pulled it on before leaving the room. A rough laugh blossomed in his chest as he realized Penelope's anger over his confession had helped him. At least now, he did not have to worry about making a clean break with her in order to continue pursuing marriage to someone else. He would likely go on to wed Cassandra Lane, and she ... well, he had no notion what Penelope would do. She had made it quite clear that as of now, that was none of his concern.

He tried to ignore the ache in his chest as he descended the stairs to the first floor.

It proved impossible.

CHAPTER 15

*P*enelope swiped at the tears coursing down her cheeks, glaring daggers at the pitiful reflection in her vanity mirror. Half an hour after her return from Edmond's house, and she couldn't seem to stop crying.

"He is wrong," she told herself. "I don't care ... I care nothing for either of them."

Her red, swollen eyes, and blotchy cheeks begged to differ. Damn Edmond! Damn both he and Colin to Hell! How was a woman supposed to exact revenge on two men who insisted on involving softer emotions? Adding insult to injury was the fact that she'd thought herself purged from all flights of fancy and the desire for romance and love. If anything, Edmond's hypnotic story about Penelope's future had proven her wrong. He'd broken through her defenses in a way no man had in a long time—finding his way through the fissure Colin had created during their last encounter.

It felt like the vilest sort of betrayal—betrayal of self.

What was worse, she still wanted him ... desired them both, if she were being honest with herself. Both offered her something she found alluring, and both had confessed love for her. Ironic, how her worst fear as a young debutante had been ending her first Season without a single offer. Now, at the end of her fourth, she found herself faced with two very different men who both wanted her, and who also happened to be best friends.

Despite what they had done to her, she found herself missing them both—Edmond's devil-may-care nature and smiles; Colin's dry humor and familiarity. Damn them both for making her care about them, when neither deserved it!

"What are you thinking?" she whispered, glaring at herself in the mirror. "You do not need either of them. You are better off alone ... that's the way it has been all this time, and that's the way it will remain."

Swiping away the last of her tears, she squared her shoulders.

"Pull yourself together," she murmured, her voice coming a bit stronger now. "The time has come to end this."

Standing, she made her way to the escritoire in the corner of her room. Within minutes, she had penned a note to Colin, telling him she needed to see him that night. As the sun rose beyond her window, she resolved to put this entire thing behind her once and for all. She had already told Edmond to stay away; now she would do the same with Colin. Then, she would continue on about her life, setting in motion the plans she'd made for herself.

It would be safer that way.

Rising, she sealed the note. Ignoring the fatigue and emotional exhaustion that had her wanting to burrow beneath her blankets and never come out again, she rang for her abigail. Once she was bathed, fed, and had sent her note to be delivered, she would feel much better. The sun had risen on a hellish day, but she was determined that tomorrow would be brighter.

Colin was waiting up for her at midnight, as he had promised in his answer to her note. He answered the door within seconds of her knock, which lead her to believe he'd been pacing nearby. A smile curved his mouth when he saw her, yet she read something else in his gaze. Brow furrowed, he appeared to have a heavy burden weighing on his mind.

It doesn't matter, she reminded herself, stilling her shaky hands. *I don't care.*

"Your note seemed urgent," he said as he ushered her into his sitting room.

Lowering himself onto a chair, he ran his fingers through his hair.

"It is," she replied, keeping her posture rigid as she sank onto the sofa across from him. "We did not talk much last time I visited. I think it's time now."

Straightening, he widened his eyes, studying her as if trying to decipher where this conversation would be going.

"Very well," he replied. "I have spoken my mind to you, with honesty and sincerity. I hope now, you are ready to do the same."

Folding her hands demurely in her lap, she raised her chin and forced herself to meet his gaze. She would not give him any reason to think she didn't mean every word she was about to say.

"Colin, what happened the last time I was here … "

"I haven't stopped thinking about it," he supplied when she trailed off. "It was … beautiful."

Clenching her teeth, she clasped her hands together in her lap and fought to remain composed. "It was a mistake."

Colin's face fell, panic alighting in his eyes. "Penelope, no."

"Yes, it was. A mistake we cannot repeat. Sexual desire might exist between us, but that is all there is. I think we fooled ourselves into believing there was more all those years ago, but we were young and foolish. It is time for us to face reality."

He shot to his feet, hands clenching into fists at his sides.

"Don't you dare," he growled, chest heaving forcefully beneath his half-open shirt. "Don't you for one second think to tell me the state of my own heart. If you have something to say to me, then have your say

... but don't tell me I don't love you now, or that I didn't love you then."

"You *didn't* love me then," she retorted. "How could you have?"

He looked away, jaw clamping tight. When he turned back to her, he nodded as if having just decided something.

"I realize I was not exactly good at showing it as a younger man. I hurt you, and I am sorry. I don't know how else to prove that I love you, and that I've changed. No other way than to just show you."

Reaching for his shirt, he jerked it from the waistband of his breeches, then pulled it off over his head.

She drew in a sharp breath at the sight of his naked torso, golden and rippled. "What are you doing?"

Continuing to watch her with that stubborn set to his jaw, he began unfastening his breeches. Refusing to reply, he went on undressing. Penelope tried to avert her gaze, but was held captive as he revealed the rest of his body—the long legs and thick root of his cock.

But then, an anomaly caught her eye. She couldn't contain her sharp gasp at the sight of the ugly, red, veiny scars marring his left thigh. A puckered area showed her the initial injury, while the fiery tendrils reaching down toward his knee and up toward his groin showed the extent of the damage.

As determined as she had been not to let him see her cry, she could no more stop the tears from filling her eyes than she could block out the compassion causing her heart to ache.

"Oh, Colin," she whispered. "What did they do to you?"

His eyes remained wide pools of uncertainty, as if he feared her reaction to the scars. She faintly remembered him keeping his breeches on when they'd made love, and now understood why. He hadn't wanted her to see.

"Waterloo might have been counted a victory, but it was a bloody massacre, dealing heavy blows to both sides. That day ... it was unending carnage and chaos, and some parts of it pass through my memory in blurs so swift I can barely recall them. But this ..." he gestured toward his mangled thigh. "This, I remember as if it happened yesterday. Its occurrence haunts my dreams almost nightly, and the pain is a constant reminder."

Unable to help herself, she reached for him, skimming her fingertips along one of the angry red lines cutting a jagged path across his skin.

"How did it happen?" she asked.

"There was a moment when we faced a cavalry charge—thousands of them on horseback, bearing down on us with sabers raised. Wellington's maneuvers tricked them into believing we had begun to retreat. They thought to wipe us out, overwhelming us with sheer force and a bit of shock and awe. But Wellington ... by God, he is one of the most brilliant strategic minds to ever lead an army. The man knew how to best them. He arranged us, infantrymen, in box formations guarding artillery, to keep them off with the bayonets when they crashed over us like a thundering tide, then standing aside for the artillery, so they could blast them to kingdom come as they receded back to form up again. It was working ... an excellent strategy. While we lost men in each pass, we dented their numbers, as well. But then ..."

He paused, swallowing and clenching his fists to still his shaking hands. "A captain at the head of my formation turned craven. In hindsight, I cannot blame him. It takes a fearless man to stand his ground when thousands of pounds of horseflesh bear down on you, with sabers slashing down from a sea of blue coats. The man was terrified. Well, he turned tail and ran. When his men saw this, they began to retreat as well, and others observing this fell in line like an avalanche. The formations began falling like a house of cards, one by one, following the coward's lead. And I ... fool I was, I thought I could be a better leader than him. A lieutenant, brave enough to stand when a captain might flee."

"You did the right thing," she murmured. "You fought with honor."

He snorted, shaking his head. "No, Penelope, I fought like an idiot. I gathered as many men as I could and pursued to turn them back before another wave could come. And, bayonets raised with war cries on our lips, we met them head on, determined to protect the artillery from the next wave. When they came again, it was at the height of their strength, it seemed. They came with such ferocity, their horses' hooves kicking, saber's slashing. And in that instant, half of the men following me were dead, felled by sabers and pistol fire. They dropped in an eye's blink ... like so many piles of bricks."

She gasped, clapping her hand over her mouth as she imagined what he must have felt, watching so many men fall right before his eyes.

"Oh, no."

"It did not end there. As they ebbed back, I pursued, dissatisfied to wait for them to double back. Emboldened by my rash actions, many followed. We had them on the run, having sawed their numbers in half with the artillery and bayonets. All seemed to be going well, but then ... I spied a man I admired above most in danger. A rider bore down on him, saber raised to strike. Raising my bayonet, I took aim and fired, taking the man out with a shot that went through his back and out through his chest. I lowered my head for a moment to reload, leaving myself vulnerable for a short moment and ... and then, there was pain unlike anything I've ever known. A bayonet of one of my fallen comrades, in the hands of a downed French cavalryman. As he lay dying, he thought to take me with him."

Closing her eyes, she drew in a deep, slow breath, hoping to calm her trembling hands. The picture he painted became so clear, and Penelope could not escape it, even with her eyes shut.

"I retaliated with my bayonet through his throat just before I crumbled, falling into the dirt. Later, the physicians told me that the wound had occurred in a vulnerable place on my thigh ... close to a vital artery that might have caused me to bleed to death ... and I almost did. While I lay on the ground with the battle raging around me, I knew I was going to die. I could smell my own blood, my vision grew obscure, and I became numb to the pain. Yet, as I felt myself drifting further and further away, there was one thing that kept me alive—one thing I held in my mind to keep me from wanting to give up and die."

Her held breath had begun to make her chest burn, and she released it now on a sigh.

"What did you see?"

He smiled, striding forward and kneeling before her. "You," he whispered.

He reached out to cup her face, and she didn't resist, allowing him to palm her cheek, his thumb swiping away one of her tears.

"For a moment, I told myself I had no reason to live. I am a third son, unwed, and childless. No one would miss me. But then, your face appeared in my mind like a beacon, and it pulled me back to the light. I realized I couldn't die, because I had to repair what I had broken."

She shook her head, lowering her gaze. "You may have hurt me, Colin, but I am not broken."

He leaned in, pressing his forehead against hers. "No, love, I was the broken one. I had hurt you, and it had made a lesser man of me. Leaving you before our wedding was an act of cowardice, and in my mind, one act of foolish bravery on the battlefield could never be enough to atone for that. So, I told myself I couldn't die ... I *refused* to die until I had seen your face again. Until I could look you in the eye and tell you that I am lost without you. It took me running away to find that I could never truly be free of you. And once I could stand again, I vowed I would make the most of my second chance. So ... never tell me that I do not love you, Penelope. If you wish to tell me you never loved me at all, I can accept that. But this scar bears witness to my love for you. It reminds me that when I had nothing left, you were my reason to live."

Penelope sobbed, despite trying to clench her teeth around the sound. Her chest burned as she tried to hold it in, fighting it until the last thread of her will snapped. She could no more deny the state of her heart than she could deny her lungs their next breath. Just as Colin had tried to run from the truth, so had she. The last of her resistance shattered, and she reached for him, taking her face in his hands.

Chest heaving with heavy breath, she finally allowed herself to give voice to the truth.

"You wounded me, Colin ... so deeply, I thought I might die from the pain."

He nodded, clutching at her arms and holding tight. "I know ... I know, Penny. Please, forgive me. I beg you."

"The truth is, I could never have been hurt by you if I didn't love you to begin with," she continued. "So, yes, Colin ... I did love you."

He released a sigh—of relief, most probably—his hands skimming up to her shoulders, which he held and drew her closer. His warm breath caressed her cheek as he rested his lips there, just beside her mouth. Pausing, he seemed to wait for her to give him permission— for her to extend the trust to him that he had once lost.

"And now?" he murmured. "Now, Penny?"

Sighing, she sank into him, unable to deny the truth now that it lay right before her. "As much as I might have wanted to, I cannot stop loving you. Even when it hurts. Even when loving you is the stupidest thing I could ever do ... I still love you, Colin."

She hated herself for it, though she could not bring herself to tell him that bit. Because loving him felt like betraying Edmond. It felt like betraying herself. Despite that, nothing could have stopped her from lowering her head and pressing her mouth to his.

The first touch of his lips against hers sparked a flame within her that had lain dormant for three long years. She'd forgotten what it was to be kissed by him, to become swept away on his tide of possession. His lips claimed hers, his hunger and need apparent by the deep pressure of his mouth and the insistent tickle of his tongue. She opened for him, overwhelmed, flooded by his taste, his musky male scent, his strong arms plucking her from the sofa.

Penelope realized they moved, but did not care. Where he took her did not matter, so long as his kiss continued feeding her starving soul. She hadn't even known she was dying from lack of what he gave; yet, it made itself apparent now as he continued drinking from her mouth while walking her through the door to his bedroom. Despite the slight dip every other step caused by his limp, she felt secure in his hold.

Depositing her on the bed, he broke the kiss long enough to light a few candles, casting a soft, yellow glow about the room. Enthralled at the sight of him walking toward her, the firelight playing over his magnificent body, she crawled toward the edge of the bed to meet him.

She came up on her knees, pressing her hands flat against his chest. He reached out to stroke her hair, taking it in a gentle hold. He held on as she kissed her way from his throat, down to the swell of his chest. He groaned, the muscles in his abdomen bunching and flexing as she tasted him, her tongue tracing the defined lines, her lips tickling in a light caress.

His knees buckled when she reached out to touch him, her fingertips tracing the lines marring his thigh. Gazing down at her, his eyes naked with vulnerability, he watched as she smoothed her fingers over the scars, running them from his thigh up toward his groin. He flinched, causing her to pause.

"Does this hurt?" she asked.

He chuckled, reaching down to stroke her cheek. "God in Heaven, no. Your touch is a soothing balm."

Smiling, she lowered her head and placed a kiss over the place where the bayonet had impaled him. He jerked, his stomach clenching and a hiss escaping him as she continued kissing him, making her way inward toward his rapidly hardening cock. She nipped his thigh, then licked along the crease where it met his pelvis, delighting in the shivers and gooseflesh it earned her.

Grasping his cock, she brought it to her lips, gracing the swollen head with a kiss. He shuddered, clutching her shoulders and shifting to find better balance. Flicking her tongue out, she circled the tip, lapping at the iridescent bead of his seed seeping from the slit. Then, without hesitation, she opened her mouth wide and took him in as far as she possibly could. Colin cried out, his legs quivering as his cock forged a path to the back of her throat. She relaxed, closing her eyes as she began loving him with her mouth, sucking him with deep, long strokes.

"Bloody hell," he moaned, clutching the back of her neck and thrusting in time with her suctioning mouth.

She fought back a giggle as he buckled again, his legs becoming dangerously unreliable in the face of her erotic torment. Taking him in her palm, she began stroking him with a firm hand, while lowering her head to the bulging sac beneath his cock.

"Ah, Penny," he groaned as she continued teasing him, her tongue caressing his bollocks while her hand continued stroking him at a steady pace. "A man could die from such torment."

Sitting up, but still maintaining her hold on his cock, she gave him a wicked smile. "I suppose I'd better stop, then."

Tumbling her back onto the bed, he came over her with a chuckle. "Don't you dare."

His lips found hers again, engaging her in a slow, sensual dance as he busied himself with lifting her skirts. Finding her naked beneath them, her quim wet and ready, he groaned.

"I want to take my time with you, love. I want to strip you naked and kiss every glorious inch of your body before I make love to you. But it's been so long."

Spreading her legs, she arched her back, inviting him in. "Next time," she told him. "I cannot wait any longer. Take me, Colin."

"Thank God," he murmured as he entered her, not bothering with finesse.

His rough entry stoked the flames in her belly to a raging inferno, causing the heat and tension in her core to reach near unbearable limits. She screamed, wrapping her arms around his neck and holding on tight as he took up a pounding rhythm between her thighs.

Reaching up to the neckline of her gown, he jerked it down, causing her breasts to bounce free. He engaged her mouth while his hand cupped one of her tits, his thumb and forefinger taking the nipple and teasing it mercilessly. She whimpered against his lips, wrapping her legs around his waist. Trailing her hands downward, she skimmed his broad shoulders, reveling in the bunch and roll of his muscles as he strained for control—a battle he was steadily losing as his thrusts became wilder and more frenzied, his hips slamming so hard against hers that she could feel the impact of it through her entire body.

He lowered his head and took one nipple into his mouth, ravaging it with his tongue as he reached beneath her, grasping her buttocks and lifting her from the bed to change the angle of his thrusts. She screamed out in ecstasy as her climax slammed into her with the force of a hammer, stealing her breath and unfurling in her core in waves of pounding spasms. Colin kissed his way to her throat, never ceasing his steady rhythm between her thighs, his tongue stroking a path toward her jaw.

Stars danced behind her lowered eyelids as the waves seemed to go on and on, causing her heart to hammer wildly in her chest.

Rising up on his knees, Colin hooked his arms beneath her bent knees and lifted her lower body from the bed. Still inside her, he took up the mad pace again, seeming heedless that she hovered on the brink of insanity. Her climax had all but died away, yet he brought another one to life on the heels of it, his strokes forging a deep and sure path through her, his thick cock stroking her inner walls and teasing the sensitive place deep inside of her that only he seemed to know how to find.

"Colin," she whimpered, her voice a ragged, choked whisper. "I'm ... I'm ... oh, God!"

She splintered again, this ending swelling to a level of intensity rivaling the first. She arched her back, lips parting on a silent cry as her entire body seemed to tremble from within. Her sheath clenched him with a powerful grip, causing him to moan and fall against her, trembling as his own rapture ripped through him. Pulling away just in time, he spent, the warm rush of his seed heating her belly.

His breath harsh, he rolled away, seeming to search for the strength to stand. Penelope closed her eyes, heedless to her lifted skirts, spread legs, and the mess staining her stomach. At the moment, she felt buoyed, as if she could float right up to the clouds. The bed shifted when Colin left it, returning a moment later with a cold, damp cloth.

"I apologize," he murmured as he deftly cleaned her. "I should have pulled out sooner."

Studying the top of his head as he finished bathing her, she frowned. "Twice now, you've had the chance to attempt impregnating me in order to secure my promise of marriage. And twice, you showed restraint. Why?"

Placing the cloth on his bedside table, he lowered her skirts, then covered her breasts. Tucking one strand of hair behind her ear, he cupped her face and smiled.

"Because I tried winning you without honor the first time ... by compromising you. This time, I wanted you to come to me on your own. No tricks, no intrigues ... just me winning your heart the way it should have been in the first place."

It lay on the tip of her tongue to tell him she knew about his little game with Edmond. Yet, she lacked the desire to harp on it again as she had with his friend. The truth remained that Colin loved her as he'd claimed, and she'd known that all along. He'd tried to approach her the right way at first and she had given him the cold shoulder. Could she fault him for doing whatever it took to reach her?

No, but she could blame him for putting Edmond in her path. Even as he drew her into his arms and lay back against the pillows, she thought of him—his mournful green gaze fixed upon her as he declared his love.

Could she blame him for what had occurred between them?

No, she realized. That, too, had been her fault. The flirtation had been initiated by her. Perhaps his will should have been stronger; however, Penelope did not stand in a position to judge him for being weak-willed when she'd been appallingly pathetic herself.

"Colin ... there is more we need to discuss," she whispered. "Things I must tell you."

Kissing the top of her head, he rested his chin there, tightening his arms around her.

"Tomorrow," he murmured, his voice thick with drowsiness. "You are exhausted; I can hear it in your voice. It's been an eventful night, and I want you to sleep a bit before I take you home."

Tomorrow ... yes, tomorrow would be soon enough. Somehow, she had to find a way to convince Edmond he did not love her. She would marry Colin, after all, and it was best if he married his heiress. What had passed between them would be forgotten in time, she felt certain. Yes, this was for the best.

Why then, did the very thought of permanently severing herself from Edmond to choose Colin leave her feeling as if she would be violently ill? Yet, when she pondered the reverse—spurning Colin to choose Edmond—the feeling did not abate. No matter which man she chose, she felt as if she cut away a piece of her heart.

As Colin drifted off to sleep beneath her, she pressed the back of her hand to her mouth to stifle the sound of her sobs.

What have I done?

CHAPTER 16

Colin removed his mask, using one arm to mop the sweat from his brow. Lowering the point of his epée, he gave Edmond a sly smile.

"That makes five points, meaning I've bested you for two bouts now. What's the matter, old chap? Did you have a bit too much to drink last night?"

Removing his mask as well, Edmond shook his head, sending beads of sweat flinging off his damp locks. He looked a fright, and despite shaking his head in response to Colin's question, seemed as if he'd spent the night before drowning in spirits. Pale skin, lips tight and drawn, dark circles beneath his eyes—which were bloodshot.

He'd had to coerce his friend into leaving home to join him for an afternoon of sparring at Angelo's School of Arms, London's most exclusive fencing club for gentleman. Colin had hoped the activity would lift Edmond's spirits, yet it became clear to him that his chum remained in a dudgeon for reasons he could not discern.

"Another bout?" he asked, twirling his epée with expert flair.

"I believe I am quite finished, thank you," Edmond muttered, striding over to a nearby bench and sinking onto it. Laying his epée across his knees, he removed his gloves and ran another hand through his hair.

Colin joined him, resting his elbows on his knees, turning the point of his weapon down toward the floor. Pressing it between his palms, he rubbed his hands together, twirling the blade, watching it gleam. It seemed he had no notion of how to talk to Edmond these days. Distance had grown between them, and he hadn't the slightest idea why.

He almost felt guilty for his downright giddy mood and the influx of energy that had him feeling like a lad again. Even the twinges of pain in his thigh couldn't rob him of the exhilaration he felt following a night of bliss with Penelope. His plans for the future were finally beginning to fall into place. Just before sunrise, he'd escorted her home, and she'd agreed to come to him again that evening so they could continue their discussion from the previous night; at which time, he'd decided to tell her about the position he'd been offered at the War Office.

This time, he decided with a smile, he would keep his hands off her tempting little body until after the talking was done. It would be bloody hard, but they had the rest of their lives for making love. The thought widened his grin until he felt certain he looked akin to a Cheshire cat.

"What the devil has you grinning like an idiot?" Edmond grumbled, smoothing a hand over his haggard face.

He laughed. "Sorry. It's just … well, I think things with Penelope have finally fallen into place."

Edmond seemed to perk up at that, straightening and wrinkling his brow. "They have?"

"We've been seeing each other in secret. At first, she seemed reluctant to hear me out—though I could hardly blame her. But now … well, I do believe a wedding might cap the Season."

Lifting his eyebrows, Edmond seemed to experience shock at his declaration. "You've proposed? She accepted?"

Puzzled by Edmond's reaction to his news, he scowled. Perhaps it was talk of marriage that caused it. After all, the Season might bring him a bride, as well—one he barely knew and probably did not like much.

"Not yet, but I will," he replied. "Our recent conversations have led me to believe she will accept. I thought it was foolish to hope she might still love me after what I'd done, but ... well, it wasn't such a forlorn hope, after all."

Edmond nodded, lowering his head with a sigh. "Providing she accepts, at any rate."

Straightening his spine, Colin inclined his head. "I say, Ed. What in hell has gotten into you?"

Standing, Edmond collected his epée, mask, and gloves. "Nothing. I'm exhausted, is all. Sleepless nights and anxiety over an impending, unwanted marriage will do that to a fellow."

Colin stood, as well. "Of course. I understand, it's just ... well, if there is anything I can do—"

"Here's something, for a start," he snapped, turning to walk away. "Realize that not everything can be about you all the bloody time, Colin."

Remaining where Edmond had left him, he felt the sting of his friend's words, as well as a bit of annoyance. He realized the man endured a difficult time at the moment, but he was not to blame. Besides, he'd tried many times to get Edmond to open up to him about what had him in such a mood. His friend had remained closed tighter than a clam clutching a pearl.

Having known Edmond since he was a lad, Colin understood him as well as he did his own self. Something was wrong, and he hid something.

Striding resolutely after Edmond, he vowed to discover what.

Returning the borrowed equipment, he quickly dressed and groomed himself back into the picture of a respectable gentleman. Stepping out onto Bond Street, he spied Edmond disappearing into the crowd, walking at a brisk pace. Determined to get to the bottom of this, he set off after him, careful to keep his distance.

It proved easy while on Bond Street—which had come alive for the day, filled with shoppers and the peacocks preening for the benefit of being seen. After a few turns, he became forced to hang further back, lurking in shadowed alleys while peering out to determine Edmond's direction. Eventually, they arrived in Grosvenor Square, and Colin realized he might have followed him for nothing. Edmond simply walked home.

But then, he set foot on Brook Street, and Colin felt his heart drop into his stomach. Penelope lived with her parents at 39, Brook Street. What the devil could he want with her?

Ducking into the alley between two houses, he leaned against its side, his mind a whirl of chaotic thoughts. Why would Edmond visit Penelope minutes after discovering he meant to propose to her? He realized the two might have formed a friendship of sorts during the time Edmond had set about persuading her in Colin's direction. Perhaps he had come to confirm for himself that his help would no longer be needed. Still, Colin could not leave until he knew for sure.

Uncertain how long he waited, he paced the narrow alley, peeking out into the street every now and then to watch for Edmond. Eventually, the door to Penelope's house opened, and she appeared on Edmond's arm dressed for walking. His hand curled into a fist as he realized they strolled in his direction. Pressing himself back against the side of the house, he waited until they passed, oblivious to his presence.

They did not talk, yet he noticed an air of familiarity that set his teeth on edge. They walked too close to each other, Edmond's hand over hers where it rested in the crook of his arm possessive.

What the devil went on between them?

Following them, hat pulled low, he kept his eyes on their backs. They walked for several blocks before Edmond suddenly paused, snatching Penelope off the street and into an alley between two rows of townhouses. Beyond them, the mews stretched, the scent of horse, hay, and manure lingering in the air. As he stood in the mouth of the alley watching them, his gut contracted, forcing bile up into his throat at the sight of Edmond pressing Penelope up against the brick facing of one house with his body and claiming her mouth in a kiss.

His lunch threatened to make a reappearance as she went limp in his arms, as if unable to help herself, returning the intimacy.

Despite the rage clouding his vision, and the urge to go stomping down the alley and snatch them apart before beating Edmond to a pulp, Colin held himself in check. Taking advantage of their closed eyes, he crept closer, ducking into the gap between two houses and crouching behind the back stairs. Peering over the stone balustrade, he choked back the urge to become violently ill and watched.

Edmond savored the feel of Penelope on his lips, the taste of her on his tongue. If Colin could be believed, this might be the last time he'd experience it. To his surprise, she accepted his kiss, returning it with her own fervor.

He hadn't thought she would receive him, or accept his invitation for a walk—yet, she must have realized, as he did, that they faced unfinished business. Despite the words she'd hurled at him during their last encounter, he had discerned the truth: Penelope was afraid. Even if she didn't love him, he had broken through her defenses. She felt *something* for him.

Yet, this news about Colin did not bode well for him. The small hope he'd held that he might earn her love had been dashed by his best friend's declaration, as if he'd been doused in the face with cold water. He was losing her, desperation becoming a churning maelstrom in his gut.

Pulling away, he cupped her face, staring down at her. "I saw Colin today."

Her widening eyes and trembling chin confirmed his worse fear. She lowered her gaze, but did not step away from the circle of his arms, nor did she attempt to place any distance between their bodies.

"Edmond ... I'm so sorry."

His chest began to ache. "So, it's true. He's won you back."

She sighed, shaking her head. "You must not think of it that way. I am not a prize to be won."

Tracing a slow circle on her cheek with his thumb, he sank against her, pressing his pelvis against hers. "No, Penny, you are *the* prize. The only woman I've ever loved."

She trembled as if his words physically affected her. "Please ... please stop saying that."

Refusing to back down, he leaned in until his lips grazed her jaw. His cock hardened due to her proximity, begging for entrance into her body.

"Why?" he murmured. "Because the truth is too difficult for you to bear?"

Meeting his gaze, she sighed. "Yes. It is like torture, Edmond. I *cannot* love you back."

His heart seemed to stop beating, and he drew in a sharp breath. She hadn't said she did not love him ... she'd stated she *could not*.

"I know that you love Colin," he said, his heart breaking even as he said the words. "But if there is even the slightest chance that you might love me, too, just a little ... then I can't walk away. Not until I've begged you to be mine."

She gasped, pressing her hands against his chest. "Edmond!"

"Just answer me, Penelope," he insisted. "I need to know the truth. What do you feel for me?"

She stared up at him, lips parted, gaze uncertain. For a long moment, she did not speak, and Edmond feared she never would. But he *needed* her to.

"I loved him first," she whispered. "That is why what I feel for you seems like betrayal. At first, I thought to use you against him— revenge for what he'd done to me. I thought of you as a plaything, the same way many men have thought of me as one. But you showed me who you really are, Ed—a sweet, kind, generous man who wants to be loved. How could a woman not lose her heart to someone like you?"

"Then ... you do love me?"

Her lower lip trembled again, as if she might cry, yet she did not. Drawing a deep breath, she nodded.

"I do love you."

With a hoarse cry, he grasped her waist and lifted her, pressing her to the wall. He took her mouth again, ravaging it without restraint. She whimpered against his lips, sliding her hands from his chest, over his shoulders, up his neck, tangling her fingers in the overgrown strands of his hair. His groin grew painful, his cock at full mast, pressing insistently against her belly. The strength of her declaration seemed to have fueled his desire, turning it into a living thing that required satisfaction … demanded it, in fact … now.

She didn't fight him when he fisted her skirts, hurriedly lifting them. Her breath became rapid, tickling his neck as she buried her face there, holding on for dear life as he lifted her. Wrapping her legs around his waist, she clung to him as he fumbled between them to free his cock. His knuckles brushed the curls blanketing her mons, becoming drenched in her wetness. Groaning at the feel of her—hot, wet, and pulsating—he braced one hand against the brick and buried himself to the hilt. He opened his eyes to meet her gaze, never breaking it as he began to move, groaning at the feel of her, dripping wet and soaking his cock and bollocks in her sweet honey.

Lifting his other hand, he watched her pupils widen, making her eyes go dark as he ran his tongue along the knuckles, lapping up every sweet drop she'd left there. She whimpered at the sight, trembling as he fucked her, thrusting her against the wall with every movement of his hips.

Leaning into her, he latched onto her neck, tracing it with his tongue, suckling and biting, causing her to cry out. Clapping one hand over her mouth to silence her, lest someone hear them, he reached down to cup her arse with the opposite hand, guiding her up and down his cock with a force that only made her moan more against his palm. She dug her heels into his tailbone, grasping his shoulders and riding him, meeting his pace with her own frenzied need.

When she shattered, shuddering in his arms while her cunt

squeezed him with the force of her climax, he replaced his hand with his mouth, stifling her screams with a brutal kiss. She clung to him, the walls of her channel urging him on toward his own ending with powerful spasms that left him breathless.

He fumbled in his pocket for a handkerchief, producing it just in time. Reaching beneath her, he disengaged from her body, gripping his cock in the linen just before he spent.

"Ah ... fuck!" he growled as his legs quaked, his equilibrium stolen by the forceful climax.

He used his arm to brace them on the wall while Penelope climbed down off him, lowering her skirts while he cleaned himself. While fighting to catch his breath, he continued using his arm to hold himself up, certain she had milked every ounce of strength from him in an instant.

Once certain he could trust his legs again, he pocketed the handkerchief. Then, crossing the space between them, he took her face in his hands again, leaning down to kiss her. He took his time this instance, devouring her lips and engaging her tongue with gentle, slow strokes. When he'd finished, he pulled away and met her gaze.

"Marry me," he whispered.

She started, clearly frightened. He'd known it would scare her, yet could not hold it back any longer. The need to strike while the iron was hot had urged him to act.

"Edmond ..."

"Don't answer now," he added. "I just wanted you to know what I want for us. I want to see you walking toward me down the aisle of St. George's. I want to speak vows to you in front of God and the *ton*, so everyone knows you are mine. I want to take you home and make you my viscountess—and someday my countess. I want the life I dreamt of for us ... the one I know you once dreamt for yourself. We can have it all, Penelope."

"What of Miss Lane?"

He shrugged. "We have danced, and I have paid calls ... we have walked in Hyde Park. I've danced enough attention on her that she would accept my suit if I offered for her. I could marry her, and live with a virtual stranger, perhaps visit her chambers once a month to attempt siring an heir. But that is not what I want. If you say yes, Cassandra becomes no more than a distant memory, and I am certain she will make a match with someone else."

She bit her lower lip. "I ... I need time, Edmond."

He nodded. "I understand. Come, I'll walk you home. When you are ready with an answer, I will be waiting."

Taking her arm, he led her from the alley. They finished the short walk in silence, Edmond's steps lighter than they had been upon arrival. He left her at her doorstep with a kiss on her hand, after securing her promise to call on him when she'd made her decision.

Trotting down her front steps, he shoved his hands down into his pockets, making his way home. The short walk gave him just a few minutes to relive the encounter with Penelope. It seemed a bit callous to take her in an alley like a Covent Garden whore, but she was no delicate flower. A woman who gave as good as she got, he knew she enjoyed adventure and spontaneity. If she accepted his proposal, he would test the limits of her passionate nature frequently. Just the thought of having her to himself caused him to smile. No more clandestine meetings. No more guilt or shame. No more hiding.

Arriving home to an empty house, he allowed himself to rest easy. His parents had left for the country, where he hoped his father intended to take the time to evaluate his destructive behavior. Perhaps, a new man would return next spring, and everything would be all right.

Feeling better than he had in days, he removed his coat and hat, allowing a footman to take them. Meeting him in the foyer, the butler executed a stiff bow.

"My lord, Captain Worthing arrived a few minutes ago. I told him you were not at home, but he insisted upon waiting. Since you are close friends, I took the liberty of allowing it."

His good mood plummeted, and the guilt returned. He'd forgotten one little eventuality. If Penelope said yes to him, it would destroy Colin. Their friendship would never be repaired.

Damn and blast it all.

He forced a smile for his butler, who had no notion of what went on, or that the last person Edmond wanted to see at the moment was Colin.

"Very good. Where is he?"

"I escorted him to the library, my lord, and provided him with refreshment in the form of a fine brandy."

Nodding, he strode toward the door to the aforementioned room. "Thank you."

Swinging the door open, he entered without hesitation. No use in stalling; Colin could be persistent when he put his mind to it, and Edmond knew the man had sensed his foul mood earlier. He'd probably come for an explanation.

Finding the room empty, he frowned, turning his head to search for Colin. Nothing could be found but neat rows of books and plush, overstuffed furniture. Frowning, he spun in a circle, just in time to meet the fist racing toward his face.

It made impact with his jaw, catching him off guard and throwing him off balance. He staggered back into the room, fighting to regain his footing.

"You son of a bitch!"

Colin came into view, limping toward him on his walking stick, fury contorting his features. As he took another swing, Edmond lowered his hands and let it come. He deserved this, and well he knew it. If this was the penance he must pay for Penelope, then he would.

The carpet met his back after the second blow threw him off his feet, and as Colin tossed his walking stick aside and knelt over him, fist cocked back to strike again, Edmond steeled himself to take whatever was dished out.

CHAPTER 17

Colin's rage had reached the boiling point the moment he'd laid eyes on Edmond. While he had only intended to plant him one facer, once his knuckles connected with the other man's jaw, satisfaction had swelled within him. He'd needed to do it again, to punish the source of his muddled emotions. Anger, that Edmond would betray him. Sadness, that he only owned half of Penelope's heart, when he'd thought she'd given him her all. Confusion, at having witnessed the two of them making love and being unable to look away. That infuriated him most of all, that a part of him had enjoyed watching another man with a woman he thought of as his.

It became clear by the third punch that Edmond would put up no resistance, which stole the wind from his sails. If the man wasn't going to fight back, then Colin was just beating him, and the satisfaction of that only lasted for a moment. What he'd wanted was a row, something Edmond seemed determined not to give him.

"Get up," he growled, moving from on top of Edmond and reaching for his walking stick, using it to find purchase so he could pull himself to his feet. "Stand and face me, you coward."

Groaning and using his sleeve to stifle the blood streaming from a cut on his lip, Edmond struggled to sit.

"I'm not going to fight you, Colin," he murmured, his voice contorted by a lip that had begun to swell.

Heat blossomed in his face and neck as he began to pace, his knuckles turning white around the head of his cane.

"Why not? Are you so afraid to fight a cripple?"

Shaking his head, Edmond stood, not bothering to right his rumpled clothes. Pulling his arm away from his face, he studied the blood staining his shirt cuff and grimaced.

"Are you finished? If not, don't worry, I could weather more. Come on, do your worst."

"I'm not going to beat you while you lie on the rug wallowing in self-pity, turning me into the villain in this farce."

Edmond scoffed, crossing the room to the sideboard. Pouring himself a liberal splash of brandy, he downed it in one gulp, wincing as the liquor seemed to sting his lip.

"No, I think it's clear who the real villain here is. The white knight returns from war to claim his princess, sending the black knight ahead of him to smooth the way. The black knight kidnaps the princess, taking her for himself. I won't even offer an excuse for my behavior, as we both know nothing I could say will convince you that I never meant for any of this to happen."

Colin's hand curled into a fist at his side. "I am certain you fought most valiantly, but once your prick accidentally penetrated her cunt, you became ensnared and from there, it became a matter of simple biology."

"I love her."

His declaration hurt just as badly now as it had hearing it in the alley. It settled in his gut, causing him to feel as if he would become ill all over the Persian rug beneath his boots. Gripping the tumbler he'd been drinking from before Edmond's arrival, he hurled it across the room with a grunt. The satisfying sound of it shattering echoed through the room in concert with the crackling fire.

"She was mine!" he bellowed, the tendons in his neck stretched to their limit from the force of it. "You pilfered her from me like a pick-pocket … like a thief in the night. And what's worse, you didn't even possess the bollocks to come to me yourself and tell me what you'd done. No, you stoop to sneaking around behind my back, fucking her in alleys and whispering words of love, knowing all the while that it would rip my heart out."

Edmond lowered his gaze. "She knows about how we set out to trick her into marrying you. We hurt her, and this was her retaliation. We deserved it … you know we did."

"I did what I did out of desperation," he retorted. "Because you were my best friend, and I thought I could trust you to help me. You *knew* I needed her. You *knew* I was desperate. Once you knew she was on to us, you should have told me so I could mend it. I could have at least tried to make her see that what we did was necessary."

Edmond clenched his teeth as if angry, but pinched his lips together. Despite his earlier contrition, Colin sensed he held back now, likely because he'd been caught red-handed.

"You may as well say what you mean to say," he snapped. "You're dying to speak, I know you."

Edmond laughed, a harsh, rough sound. "Necessary, you say? You have some nerve. Despite being only a third son, you possess an astounding amount of arrogance and surety about the place you think you occupy in the world. You were gone for *three years*! You ruined her before you ran away like a dog with its tail tucked between its legs, yet somehow, you expected to claim her as if she'd waited for you breathlessly all this time."

"I did not—"

"You did!" Edmond insisted. "You bloody well did! You're so sure of yourself, that you assumed she would just fall into your arms as if none of it had ever happened. What you did broke that woman … so much that she doesn't even know how to love anymore. And when someone else comes along to show her, you just can't stand the fact that it isn't you! You cannot abide the thought that she might care for someone who isn't you!"

Colin flared his nostrils as he fought to control his breathing. As it was, he felt as if the rage choked him, making it difficult to breathe properly. Every word fell on him like the lash of a whip. Had he really done what Edmond claimed? Perhaps. And maybe he *was* arrogant, but that did not change the fact that Edmond had attempted to steal Penelope right out from under him without even giving him the courtesy of telling him he stood in the race for her affection.

"Say what you will, but I love her. I know her in ways you never could. In the end, that is what will win her, and if that doesn't, the fact that you're as hungry for her fortune as you are for her cunt will do the trick."

The blow came unexpected, yet as Colin fell off balance from the force of Edmond's fist against his nose, he welcomed the pain. It proved a momentary distraction from his other, inner agony. Edmond stood over him with an extended hand, offering it to him.

"That was unnecessarily low. Otherwise, I wouldn't have done that."

Swatting his hand aside, he made his way to his feet on his own, glaring at Edmond as blood trickled from one nostril.

"Did I strike a nerve?"

Edmond glowered at him with eyes burning with fury. "You may blame me for this, and call me every foul name you can think of because I know I deserve it. But never again will you insinuate that I am after her inheritance. I would want her if she were penniless."

Whipping out his handkerchief, he applied pressure to stop the bleeding, wincing at the tenderness of his nostrils and the cartilage above it. Thankfully, it did not appear to be broken.

"How convenient for you that she happens to come with heavy pockets."

When Edmond didn't respond, he turned to leave, leaning wearily on his walking stick. The upset had caused his thigh muscles to tighten, his knee to throb.

"I intend to fight you for her, Edmond. And I intend to win."

Edmond shrugged. "We both know who she will choose, and that I hardly stand a chance. You'll receive no opposition from me. She knows the state of my heart ... there is nothing more I can do."

Colin limped out of the room, not bothering to respond to Edmond's final remarks. If he did, he might be forced to admit being intimidated by his friend. As well as he knew them both, he realized what he'd seen between them in the alley had been genuine. Edmond was not a man who would tell a woman he loved her unless he meant it. He'd watched Penelope struggle with herself up until the moment she'd confessed to loving Edmond back. He saw what it cost her to admit it, even as he knew she loved him, as well.

As sure as he'd been that he had secured her as his wife, Colin now felt unease in his gut. Edmond was the kind of man women fell head over heels in love with, losing all their good sense. He was everything Colin was not, and his past history with Penelope put him in a vulnerable position. Unlike him, Edmond had never wounded her.

As he began the long walk home, it struck him that he might be the one who didn't stand a chance.

Penelope stared dismally into her tea, unable to take a single sip. She merely held the cup for the sake of its warmth seeping into her palms. She stood in an impossible situation, and had no notion of how to extract herself. Two men who loved her—whom she loved back. Both wanted to marry her. Oh, Colin had not asked her yet, but had more than made his intentions known. She fully expected him to propose when she visited him this evening as they'd arranged.

As it was, she hardly knew how she would endure the meeting, so wrung dry was she from her time with Edmond just a few hours ago. His declaration of love made for the second time shocked her far less than his proposal. Surely, he must know what a marriage between them would do to Colin. That he'd asked her anyway meant he truly did love her—enough to risk destroying their friendship. She'd never imagined anyone could love her so much. Yet, both men had demonstrated a devotion that touched her in her deepest of places. Colin, who had lived for her, and Edmond, who was willing to risk one of the most important relationships in his life for her.

How could she ever choose?

"Penelope, dearest, are you all right?"

Tearing her gaze away from the murky depths of her teacup, she glanced up to find both her parents staring at her. They'd been sharing a quiet afternoon over tea, content to do so until dinner and the ball that would cap their evening. Penelope hardly felt like going with so much weighing on her mind.

It was her mother who'd asked the question, eyeing her over her embroidery frame with concern in her gaze. The marquis lowered the book he'd been reading and studied her with a frown.

"Yes, I'm fine," she insisted, trying to inject a bit of cheer into her voice. "Just ... woolgathering."

She took a sip of tea beneath their watchful eyes and forced a smile.

"Are you feeling poorly?" Hartford asked, continuing to observe her even after her mother had gone back to her embroidery. "Perhaps you should skip the ball tonight to rest. You've seemed out of sorts all week."

Before she could offer protest, the door to the drawing room opened to admit the butler who bowed and cleared his throat with an anxious glance in the marquis' direction.

"Captain Worthing, for Lady Penelope."

At the announcement, her mother gasped, Penelope choked on a mouthful of tea, and while she sputtered and coughed, Hartford leapt to his feet with fists curled.

"Now, see here, Worthing," he blustered as Colin entered the room, leaning more heavily on his cane than usual. "I thought I told you to sod off."

Gasping, Penelope came to her feet at the sight of him, knuckles bruised, a bluish-black stain spreading from the bridge of his nose out toward his eyes.

"What's happened to you?" she blurted before she could think better of it.

Hartford strode forward, blocking Colin from her with his bulky body. "It will be nothing compared to what I'll do to him if he doesn't vacate the premises immediately."

To his credit, Colin didn't bat an eyelash when he turned his gaze to the marquis.

"I beg your pardon, my lord, but I must speak with Penelope … alone."

"Absolutely not," the marquis protested. "Now, kindly remove yourself before I have you tossed down the front steps!"

"Wait!" she cried, rounding Hartford and placing herself at Colin's side. "Papa, let him stay. I want to hear him out … please."

Colin cast her a thankful glance, while her stepfather watched her as if she'd sprouted a second head.

Placing a hand on his arm, she stood on tiptoe to kiss his weathered cheek. "Papa, I know you only want to protect me, and I love you dearly for it. But I have nearly reached my majority, and I believe I am ready to start making these sorts of decisions for myself. Don't you?"

Grunting in grudging agreement, he took a step back and nodded. "Very well. Come along, dear. Let's give them the room."

She locked gazes with her mother, who silently asked if she would be all right. Penelope gave her a nod and a smile, understanding her mother's concern. Nodding back, as if satisfied, she took Hartford's arm and allowed him to lead her from the parlor.

Once the door had closed behind them, she gestured toward the tea service. "Would you care for—"

"I know about you and Edmond," he blurted in a rush.

Hands trembling, she fought to still them by clasping her skirts and balling her fists around them. "He told you?"

Scoffing, he rolled his eyes skyward. "That bastard would never have been so brave. No, I saw you with him … this afternoon. I noticed he acted a bit odd and followed him, thinking that whatever had him feeling so low might be something I could help him with. Imagine my shock when I witnessed him helping himself … to you."

She closed her eyes and shame washed over her at the thought of him forced to watch her and Edmond. It could not have been easy for him.

"Colin I … I don't know what to say other than I'm sorry. Things were never supposed to happen this way."

Pacing away from her, he gazed through a nearby window. "That's what he said."

Blinking back tears, she became overwhelmed with grief at the thought that she might lose him for good.

"Colin, please … I know I have no right to ask you to forgive me—"

"But I do," he murmured, turning to face her. "Don't you understand that there is nothing you could do that I would not forgive? What must I do to prove that to you?"

Coming away from the window, he braced himself on his walking stick and sank down to one knee. His expression remained solemn as he gazed up at her.

"Must I kneel before you, and tell you that I cannot live without you? That I understand your hurting me was a direct result of me hurting you? From this day forward, our slate is clean. If you can forgive me, then know I have already forgiven you for this or anything else you might do … because I love you, Penny. I want to make you my wife."

She reached out to touch his face, then smoothed her fingertips up in his hair. "You are the man I always thought you were. Of course I forgive you. I love you … but you must know that I love him, as well. It isn't fair to you, Colin, nor to him."

"I don't care," he declared. "I understand that things happened and your feelings are fresh. You don't have to give your answer now. I realize you have his offer to consider, as well. Just know that I don't care about anything that has happened before this moment. If you choose me, I will love you so ardently, you'll never think of him again."

Rising once more, he smoothed his rumpled clothes. Reaching out, he stroked her cheek with his bruised knuckles, then drew her to him for a sweet, chaste kiss. Despite the kiss's quickness and lack of erotic finesse, Penelope felt it down to her very soul.

"You should know that I've taken a position with the War Office, under Major-General Sir Henry Torrens. I'm only his ensign, but there is opportunity for advancement."

She smiled. "Colin, how wonderful! I am glad for you."

He nodded, returning her smile. "I did it for us, Penny. I wanted a secure future ... to support you on my own, without help from my family. I wanted a purpose beyond that of war, which is far behind me."

Before he turned to leave, she caught hold of his sleeve.

"I recant my previous statement," she whispered. "You are a far greater man that I thought you were."

Taking her hand and kissing it, he turned to leave once and for all. She lowered herself into the closest chair, pressing both hands over her mouth and closing her eyes. She remained that way, still as death, until the sound of the front door closing and Colin's footsteps down the front stairs told her he was gone.

The marquis re-entered the room a moment later, his face drawn and grave. "Well? What did the cur want? What has he done now?"

She stood, but avoided his gaze. Hartford knew her too well, and she couldn't risk that he might see the truth in her eyes.

"He has asked me to marry him ... truly, this time."

From the corner of her eye, she spied the marquis's eyes widening just before he clenched his jaw.

"What did you say?"

"I told him I would consider it, but ... I don't believe I will accept."

As she brushed past her stepfather, she noted the look of satisfaction that passed across his face at her declaration. However, it only caused her heart to sink further and further into her stomach.

It was an impossible decision. Either way, one of them would suffer, and Penelope realized she didn't have the heart to inflict that on them. She could never find happiness with one, knowing she had broken the heart of the other.

CHAPTER 18

Colin watched the brick façade of Edmond's townhome from across the street, puzzled as to why he was here. A few days after his row with his former best friend, Penelope had sent him a note asking her to meet him here. The dead of night had fallen, and he couldn't imagine what she might want with both of them. He certainly had nothing left to say to Edmond after his betrayal. Penelope had been far easier to forgive ... as far as his supposed friend was concerned, he doubted he could ever trust the man again.

He'd spent the past couple of days closeted away at home, nursing his wounds—both physical and emotional—in private. The bruising across his nose had begun to dissipate, and he hoped the ugly mottling of yellow and green would vanish by the time he would report to the War Office for duty in three days.

Turning to glance down the lane, he spied a hansom cab barreling toward him through the night. Pulling to a stop in front of Edmond's house, it opened to reveal Penelope, shrouded in black, her head and face covered by her hooded cloak. Crossing the street, he met her before the front steps, taking her arm to assist her up to the front door.

"Why are we here, Penny?" he asked as she raised her hand to the doorknocker.

Pausing with one hand on the brass fixture, she turned to stare at him. In the shadows of her hood, her face appeared worn, her eyes ringed with dark circles. She looked as if she'd hardly slept.

"Because I have things I must say to both of you, and I do not believe I could do it twice."

Her words set a tight knot of anxiety working in his gut. Had she decided already, then? This must be it … by the end of the night, one of them would claim Penelope forever. The other … well, he tried not to think of that. He hoped not to land on the wrong side of her decision.

After a short while, Edmond came to the door himself in a state of dishabille—barefoot, no cravat or waistcoat, hair tousled. He looked as horrid as Penelope—as wretched as he supposed he must appear.

"Wonderful," he murmured, backing away from the door to allow them entrance. "Everyone's here. Let the breaking of hearts commence."

Colin glared at him over the top of Penelope's head, but Edmond merely shrugged and went back to avoiding his gaze.

"Shall we adjourn to the library?" he asked, gesturing toward the open door.

He allowed Penelope to precede him, then followed. Edmond entered last, closing and locking the door behind them, leaving the key in its hole.

Penelope moved to stand near the fire, extending her hands to soak in its warmth. Colin idled near the door, uncertain of how to proceed. She had arranged this meeting; it rested on her to guide them.

Edmond crossed the room, leaning against the desk and folding his arms across his chest. He watched Penelope as closely as Colin did, likely for some sign of what this could be about.

Eventually, she lowered her hood and turned to face them, hands clasped tightly in front of her.

"Thank you both for meeting me. I realize I have no right to ask anything of either of you ... and I appreciate you putting your differences aside for me."

Lowering her gaze, she paused to draw a deep breath. Releasing it on a sigh, she cleared her throat and continued.

"In fact, your differences are the reason we're here. You see, I have spent the last three days thinking over both your proposals. I vow, no woman could ever be as conflicted as I have been. Colin, you were my first love, and what we share is so very special. You are kind, thoughtful, passionate ... everything a woman could want. Edmond, you're witty, charming, and sweet ... again, everything any woman could ask for. I do not believe I could ever deserve either of you."

"Penelope, you are unlike anyone I have ever known," Edmond said, gaze cast downward at his bare feet. "It is I who is not worthy."

Colin inclined his head. "On that, we agree."

When Edmond's head snapped up in surprise, Colin raised a hand in defense.

"I was referring to myself," he amended.

"It occurred to me that I cannot choose," she said, her voice growing hoarse. "Because whoever I choose, the other man will be hurt. But, more than that, your friendship will be forever ruined, irreparably. That breaks my heart most of all, to know that you two may never speak to each other again ... that your camaraderie has been destroyed by this. It is all my doing, and I regret so much what I have done. Please, forgive each other and be friends again. I am not worth all this fuss."

Colin felt as if he'd been punched in the gut. "Penelope ..."

While he fumbled for words, Edmond straightened, taking a step toward her.

"What are you saying?"

"I'm saying I am not choosing," she said, raising her chin. "If I must choose, then I choose your friendship over my own needs. I can't be responsible for breaking you apart."

"You are not responsible for that," Edmond argued. "I am. If you need to place blame somewhere, lay it at my feet. Choose Colin."

That took him by surprise, though it shouldn't have. Edmond had been convinced that she would choose Colin over him, anyway. Closing the distance between them, Penelope reached up to touch Edmond's face.

"But I love you, as well," she murmured.

The tenderness in her voice, directed toward another man, should have hurt him. Yet, for some odd reason, seeing them together like this didn't hurt as much as it had the first time. In fact, something seemed natural about it. Almost as right as he felt when she was with him.

"How could I choose which part of me to rip away?" she added. "I would be like deciding which half of my heart to live without. It is impossible, Edmond."

Turning to him, she left Edmond and came to him, taking his hands in hers.

"And I love you … just as much. It is too hard, I just … I cannot. Please don't ask me to choose. You two must choose each other. That is what I want."

She released him and moved as if to walk away, but Edmond stepped forward, trapping her between them.

"Wait," he said.

She turned to face him, placing Colin at her back. Edmond reached for her, cupping her head, his fingers gripping her hair in a tight but tender hold.

"What if, just this once, you did not have to choose?"

Penelope's back stiffened, and she gasped. Yet, Colin felt nothing but curiosity at what Edmond might say next. The same emotion he'd experienced watching them together in the alley began to creep over him, foreign and intriguing. He hardly knew how he felt about the sensation.

"What do you mean?" she asked, clearly affected by being trapped between both of them.

Edmond, he could see, enjoyed it, too. He eyed her with a predatory gleam in his eye, as if he were a lion stalking a skittish doe. Colin began to feel a bit feral himself. What the bloody hell was happening here?

"You don't want to choose," he continued. "I understand why. I think it is safe to say, neither of us is particularly excited by this news. And I would rather have half your heart than nothing at all."

"What … what are you saying?"

Edmond lowered his head and kissed her, the action pressing her closer against Colin. The feel of her soft curves against him sent blood rushing straight to his groin. His cock swelled, and he grasped her hips, pressing against the soft curve of her derrière.

This was madness. He'd never shared a woman with anyone before, yet the thought had crossed his mind once or twice before. He and Edmond had frequented whorehouses together in their youth, and he supposed if he were ever to share a woman with someone, it would be his best friend. However, his salacious imaginings of sharing some nameless, faceless whore with Edmond did not compare to this. They shared a common bond as friends, but also through this woman, who had ensnared them both so completely they would never be free.

Yes, he would do this, because there seemed to be no other choice. He felt safe in sharing her with someone he knew and trusted, someone he loved like a brother. Just now, nothing felt truer than what he experienced, sharing in their mutual love for this one woman.

"It's all right, darling," Edmond whispered, pulling away and reaching for the clasp of her cloak. "Stop fighting this."

"He's right," Colin added, helping him remove the garment. "Don't deny yourself the thing you want most. Don't deny us, either. Let us love you, Penny."

With a soft whimper, she went limp against him. "This … this can hardly be proper."

He chuckled, working at the back of her dress to open it. No, it wasn't proper at all, yet it felt stunningly right. His anger at Edmond notwithstanding, he could hardly fault the man for loving her. Hell, he himself proved incapable of getting her out of his mind, of putting her aside despite what she'd done. Perhaps Edmond had been right. Sharing her with someone else must be preferable to being without her at all.

"No, it is not," Edmond replied as her bodice sagged away from her breasts, revealing she wore no undergarments. "But it's going to feel so bloody good."

Penelope lost the ability to think beyond the things Colin and Edmond simultaneously did to her pliant body. If she'd found it difficult to resist one, she never stood a chance against two. Her every fantasy of having them both kiss her, touch her, ready her to take them both inside her body, was coming true. It all created a riot of sensation in her gut, which only increased her arousal.

Every inch of her skin tingled with awareness as they trapped her between them. While Colin kissed her neck, his open mouth and hot tongue setting her on fire, Edmond lowered his head as he drew her gown down, the fabric rasping over her nipples, causing them to harden. He took one into his mouth, while Colin's hand found the other, kneading and squeezing while he continued devouring the column of her throat. His erection, now fully hard and insistent, pressed against her arse, while Edmond's made its presence apparent against her belly. She trembled in the face of such power and raw maleness—all of it for her.

Edmond continued on his path down her body, grasping her gown and lowering it past her hips. His mouth traced a languid trail over her belly, his tongue creating slow circles that caused her to shudder in response. Grasping her wrists, Colin lifted her arms over her head. The feel of something soft whispered across her skin, and before she realized what was happening, her hands had been bound together, Colin's cravat knotted around them.

Skimming his hands over her goosebumps-riddled flesh, he traced his way back down her arms, palming her breasts. While Edmond knelt before her, parting her lower lips to expose the slick flesh of her quim, Colin tweaked her nipples, causing the stiff peaks to harden and shrink even more. When Edmond's tongue flicked out to taste her, she cried out, the sensation of both of them teasing her at once almost too much to bear. Yet, she felt as if she might die if either of them stopped. Never had she known such pleasure.

Edmond lifted one of her legs, draping it over his shoulder and keeping a firm hold on one thigh, increasing the pressure of his tongue strokes. She turned her head to meet Colin's questing mouth, hooking her bound hands behind his head, her fingers caressing his hair as their tongues met and dueled.

At her feet, Edmond continued his torture, taking the throbbing bud of her clit and sucking it between his lips. A moan burned in her throat, a climax striking her far too swiftly. They had hardly begun, and already, she felt as if she'd reached her limit.

Colin's hand circled her throat, his thumb stroking her pulse, his lips nibbling hers, while Edmond drew out the fluttering spasms of her completion with relentless determination. Moaning against Colin's mouth, she clung to him, using her tied hands to hang on, keeping herself on her feet.

When Edmond had finished, he stood and began undressing, his glittering green gaze fixated on her, his dark pupils widening and causing a primal light to glitter in the depths. Between the two of them, they managed to make her feel like the most treasured, desired woman that ever lived. God help her, she loved them both in a way even she didn't understand.

Colin took her up in his arms, crossing the room to lay her on the thick rug before the fire. Now nude, Edmond knelt at her head, the firelight caressing the taut stretches of muscle making up his perfect body. Colin, divested of his coat, shirt, waistcoat, and boots, knelt at her feet, and both men reached for her at once.

She felt like a pagan sacrifice, offered up to two gods—one dark, and one light—as Colin grasped her ankles and Edmond her wrists, stretching her out between them. Colin bent her legs and knelt between them, picking up where Edmond had left off. Sinking two fingers into her wet, beckoning sheath, he pumped them in and out while his thumb traced slow circles over her sensitive pearl.

She turned her head to find Edmond's thick cock angled toward her. Licking her lips, she raised her gaze to meet his and smiled.

"Come here," she murmured before her words broke off on a moan caused by Colin's skilled fingers.

Edmond edged closer to her, grasping her hair and guiding his cock toward her lips. She parted them, taking him in and stroking the underside of his shaft with her tongue. He groaned, his fingers tightening around her hair as his hips took up a slow thrust, sliding himself in and out of her mouth in the same rhythm with which Colin stroked her with his fingers. She sucked Edmond with deep pulls, closing her eyes and savoring his masculine scent and heady flavor.

"Will you come for us again, love?" Colin whispered, his fingers quickening inside her. "Christ, you're so wet … so close …"

Whimpering, she nodded, feeling another telltale tremor deep in her core. Pinching one of her nipples, Edmond teased her even closer.

"Yes, darling," he murmured. "That's it. Come for us."

She lifted her hips, urging Colin on harder, faster. He obliged her, slamming his fingers in deep, sheathing himself to the third knuckle, his fingers finding the secret place deep within that caused her to cry out as flashes of light and color stole her vision. Colin applied pressure to her clit with his thumb, and the pleasure of it combined with another pinch from Edmond on her tender nipple, and she spiraled, toppling over the edge.

Her lips tightened around Edmond's cock, her suckling pulls becoming more desperate, offering an outlet for the storm tearing her apart inside. Crying out, he trembled, his grasp on her hair growing tighter. She reveled in the sting, enjoying it as much as she did the pounding spasms causing her inner walls to grip Colin's fingers with shuddering contractions.

Colin tore his breeches open, kneeling between her knees and snatching his fingers free before replacing them with his cock. He slammed into her with one forceful thrust, coming fully into her until his pelvis met hers. Her cry of ecstasy became trapped in her chest, with Edmond's cock thrusting in and out of her mouth, his cadence now speeding up to match Colin's between her thighs. Over and over, they entered her, filling her and satisfying every urge at once. Four hands touched her, one of Colin's on her thigh, the other stroking her clit; one of Edmond's in her hair, the other teasing her sensitive nipples. Their hoarse moans sent a thrill through her, filling her with pride that she could be a source of such satisfaction for them both.

Penelope's climax faded, but had barely died before another came, this one far more powerful than the other two. Her back arched, her hips bowing up off the floor, pressing herself even closer to Colin, whose grip on her thigh tightened painfully in reaction as he slid even deeper into her, stroking her secret, innermost places.

Above her, Edmond began to tremble, his chest heaving as his breaths seemed to come shorter and shorter, each one emitting on a low moan. Finally, he thrust one last time with a groan, his seed flooding her palate with his primitive taste. She didn't let up, her cheeks caving in as she sucked him until the hot spurts ceased, until he looked as if he might die, his eyes closed and his face contorted into an expression of pure bliss.

Colin spent a moment later, jerking away from her and spilling into his shirt—the closest scrap of cloth he could lay hands on.

Edmond withdrew from her mouth, leaning down to kiss her before he began untying her hands. Once freed, however, all she could do was lie there and wait for her body to climb down from the rapturous heights they had both taken her to. Drowsiness pulled at the edges of her consciousness, while euphoria caused the languid sensation of floating to buoy her. And in the midst of it all, love for them both robbed her of breath.

Never had she imagined being with them both could make her feel so fulfilled—or that it would feel so perfect. It was no wonder choosing between them had been so impossible, when it felt as if she'd always been meant for both.

Edmond's hands found her shoulders, helping her to sit up.

"We've exhausted her," Colin mused, fastening his breeches.

Nodding, Edmond reached for his shirt. "I'll ensure there are no servants up and about, then you help me get her upstairs."

Penelope allowed Colin to help her into her gown, though he left it unfastened at the back. Her eyes slid closed when he lifted her in his arms, cradling her against his chest. She heard Edmond return a moment later, informing them the way was clear. Colin handed her off to Edmond to be carried up the stairs, following with his arms full of their discarded articles of clothing, including her cloak.

Once safe inside Edmond's chamber, she found herself laid on his soft bed. A moment later, Colin removed her dress once more, while Edmond draped her in one of his shirts. One laid her against the pillows while the other pulled the blankets up to her chin. Just before drifting off to sleep, she giggled.

"Whatever could you find so funny at a time like this?" Edmond asked, his tone tinged with amusement.

A smirk pulled at one corner of her mouth as she opened her eyes and peered at them, standing together at the foot of the bed.

"Oh, nothing," she mumbled. "It's just nice to see you two working together again."

CHAPTER 19

$\mathcal{E}$dmond gestured toward one of two twin armchairs facing the dying fire in his library before handing Colin one of the two tumblers of brandy he held. While Colin settled, he approached the hearth, shoveling more coal onto the embers and using the poker to stoke them back to life again. They'd left Penelope sleeping with a fresh blaze going in his room, after which Edmond had loaned Colin a shirt to replace his soiled one. Then, he'd suggested they adjourn to the library for what he supposed would be a surreal conversation. He was certain he had about as much of an idea concerning what to do about all this as Colin did.

Once he'd taken his own seat, he lifted his glass to Colin, then took a sip, sighing as he slouched in the chair.

After a short silence, he chuckled. "Who would have thought two old Eton and Cambridge chums could patch up their ruined, lifelong friendship by sharing a woman and a glass of brandy after a round of fisticuffs?"

Colin's eyes widened, then he chuckled as well, shoulders shaking with mirth. "I wouldn't exactly call it a 'round', Ed. I slaughtered you."

Arching one eyebrow, he smirked. "I let you. Besides, I did plant you one facer."

Pinching the bridge of his nose, Colin grimaced. "A bloody good one, too, by Jove."

They shared another laugh, then lapsed into silence, during which they each stared pensively into the fire. Edmond's finger twitched, tapping his signet against his glass.

"What are we going to do?" Colin mused, gaze still locked on the flames. "You and I have shared many things as friends over the years … but a woman?"

He shrugged. "She loves us both, it would seem. Lord knows I cannot understand it. I could never imagine loving anyone but her."

"Me, either," Colin agreed.

"What else can we do but share her? It's either that, or lose her."

Colin shook his head. "Do you hear yourself? That is insane. Share her for how long? One night is not the same as a lifetime, Ed. Besides, it isn't as if she could be married to us both."

His spine straightened as Colin's words sparked something in him. He turned to face his friend and smiled.

"Yes, she could."

Frowning, Colin took another drink. "What madness do you speak? No such marriage would ever be sanctioned."

Edmond rolled his eyes. "Of course not, you idiot. I don't mean a conventional marriage. I have a more … non-traditional union in mind."

Holding one hand up before Colin could object, he grinned. "Just hear me out. In public, and by society's standards, she could only ever belong to one of us. But, what if the three of us made a pact? Penelope is our wife, and we are her husbands. We will love her, protect her, lavish her with everything she could ever want. And behind closed doors, it would just be us. No one ever need know."

Colin shot to his feet, his expression not unlike the young boy who had despaired every time Edmond pulled him into some prank or another during their school days. He'd always been the daring one,

Colin more cautious. Yet, where Penelope was concerned, caution would get them nowhere.

"Are you insane? Consider what you are saying! What about living arrangements? What about servant gossip? What about our families? How would we ever explain it? And what about children? If one of us sires a child on her, who claims it? Does one of us get to be the father while the other is 'Uncle Colin' or 'Uncle Ed'? It will never work."

Grasping Colin's shoulders, Edmond halted him before he could begin pacing. "I know it sounds mad. But the alternative is life without her. There are plans to be made, and many long conversations we must endure as a trio, but … I don't know about you, but if I'm going to share a woman with someone, I'd only want to do it with my best friend. No one can love her like I do, except you."

Folding his arms across his chest, Colin lifted one hand to his chin and seemed to consider his words. "You're right, of course. Nothing about this will be easy. We will all be living a double life. But did you see her, Ed? When she was with us … she was … I've never seen her like that. Happy. Free. Loved. She came alive in our hands."

Edmond had seen all of that, just as Colin had. He'd never thought being with her could be any better, until tonight.

Extending one hand to his friend, he laughed. "So, what do you say? Will you share a wife with me, Colin?"

Batting his hand aside with a chuckle, Colin shook his head in disbelief. "I never thought I'd live to see the day a man would propose marriage to me."

"You're the only man I'd ever ask, believe me. And, for what it's worth, I am sorry for the way things all worked out. As well, I apologize for the things I said in the heat of the moment. I didn't mean any of it."

Colin shrugged. "Think nothing of it. Besides, I *can* be arrogant, so you weren't completely off the mark. I apologize, as well. I know you don't want Penelope for her money."

Draining the dregs of his brandy, Edmond set his glass aside. "Well, what now?"

Colin sat back down, crossing one leg over the other, and resting his ankle on his thigh. "We have a very confused woman to propose marriage to, but before we do, we'd bloody well better be prepared."

"You're right," he replied, taking his seat, as well. "I had not planned to sleep tonight, anyway. We have until just before dawn to wake her, propose, and return her home before anyone's the wiser."

Running a hand over his tired face, Colin sighed. "By all means, let us get on with it."

Penelope fought back a smile as she entered the drawing room just after breakfast the next morning. She expected her mother any moment, and together, they would receive the morning callers. One of them, she knew, was not coming for small talk over tea. One of them would come to ask her father for her hand. Her stomach had tied itself in knots, and she couldn't stop her hands from trembling. Anxiety wouldn't dissipate until everything had been said and done.

Despite the fear and apprehension curling in her middle, she also felt a great deal of excitement. She'd been awakened before sunrise by both Edmond and Colin, who had brought her to with kisses. Opening her eyes, she'd found Edmond's lips roaming her face and neck, and Colin's tracing a slow path from the back of her hand up her arm. Hunger had flared in her ... a yearning to have them both again, inside her, touching her, worshipping her body with two mouths and four hands. It must have shown in her eyes because Edmond had chuckled.

"Ready for us again so soon, darling?" he murmured. "There will be plenty of time for that later. For now, we must talk and there isn't much time."

After she'd come to full wakefulness, they'd joined her on the bed, Edmond on one side and Colin on the other. Together, they'd convinced her that just as much as she needed both of them, they needed her as well. So much that they wanted to share her as a wife.

The idea seemed so preposterous that she had laughed at first. Yet, the more they spoke of the idea, the more she began to believe it might be possible. Of course, there would be hardship, secrets, and perhaps some tough decisions to be made—but wasn't that the case in any marriage? At least, this way, she could be with both men she loved, and everyone could be happy.

They'd discussed the finer details as much as they could. Then, it was time for her to return home before it was discovered she had been gone all night. She'd made the ride home in Edmond's carriage, sandwiched on the seat between them, far too aware of the two powerful male bodies surrounding her. They'd walked her to the garden gate together, each taking turns kissing her good-bye.

"I cannot wait until there are no more good-byes between us," Edmond had murmured after his turn.

"That makes two of us," Colin had added before taking her in his arms next. "Just a little while longer, and all will be as we planned."

Oh, she hoped it would be. She had no reason to believe the marquis would refuse her marriage. While she knew her parents had resigned themselves to her living as a perpetual spinster, she also knew they'd secretly hoped she would change her mind concerning marriage. At this juncture, it did not matter who took her, so long as someone did.

"My, don't you look especially lovely this morning?" her mother murmured as she entered the room to find her already seated with a book.

Penelope smiled. "Thank you."

She'd taken great pains with her appearance, wearing her best white muslin morning gown, and arranging her hair in a soft chignon. Yet, she knew her appearance had been enhanced in part by Edmond and Colin. Being loved by them would put a glow on any woman's cheeks.

In the hour that passed, Penelope tried not to watch the door or listen too closely for the sound of the knocker. Two of their neighbors passed through, stopping for tea and biscuits and idle gossip. All the while, she counted the minutes that went by, each one leaving her more anxious than the one before it.

Finally, when their second visitor stood to leave, she heard another knock at the door. Heart leaping into her throat, she clenched the arms of her chair so tight, the wood might have splintered if she didn't force herself to ease her grip. As a footman opened the door to escort their guests out, she caught a glimpse of him being ushered through the foyer and toward the marquis's library.

She gasped, her heart leaping up into her throat. He looked splendid in his dove grey morning coat and buff breeches, his hair styled in just the right air of artful disarray. Turning his head as he passed, he caught sight of her through the open door and smiled, giving her a wink.

Her mother cast a curious glance into the hall. "Oh, I wonder what he could be doing here?"

Settling back in her chair, Penelope took up her cup and saucer and pretended to inspect the contents.

"He is here to talk to Papa, Mother."

"Oh? What about, I wonder."

Smiling, she watched her mother's face closely, amused to watch for the reaction to come. "It's nothing really ... he's simply come to ask Hartford for my hand in marriage."

CHAPTER 20

The day of Lady Penelope Hunt's marriage to Lord Edmond Ingham dawned bright and clear, the heat of the approaching summer a pleasant balm. It seemed the whole of the *ton* had turned out for what was being hailed as the most shocking union of the Season. Penelope Hunt, sworn spinster, joined in marriage to the best friend of the man everyone assumed she would have married after her first Season. Much gossip had made the rounds as to the circumstances of the match, yet Colin knew none of them could ever come close to the truth—which proved far more scandalous.

As he stood in St. George's at Edmond's back, Colin watched Penelope walk toward them down the aisle with his heart in his throat. She looked beautiful, in a demure, baby blue gown with a train that hung from the draped back, a silver-embroidered sheer material that trailed behind her as she walked. The pearl-encrusted bodice drew his eye to the swell of her décolletage, above which rested a pearl choker. All that vibrant red hair piled atop her head in a shower of curls showcased her heart-shaped face, one fat spiral hanging down to drape over one shoulder. Silk flowers adorned the coiffure here and there, matching those in her bouquet.

Beside him, Edmond drew a sharp breath in—he was certain—the same wonder and awe he was experiencing.

When they had first decided that Edmond would be the one to marry Penelope publicly, Colin had experienced a bit of sorrow. He could never openly declare her to be his wife. Sure, he could escort her about town, as it was par for the course for married women to spend time with men they were not wed to. When Edmond was busy, Colin would keep her company, escorting her to any engagement he could not attend with no one the wiser. Still, the thought of possibly siring a child that everyone would assume to be Edmond's, of hearing people call her by his name and title … it had stung.

It was for the best, he knew. Edmond would be an earl, and Penelope his countess. Her dowry would see his damaged estates set right, and she would give him his heir. Colin, who had no need of an heir to inherit, and a promising career with the War Office ahead of him, would live the life of a confirmed bachelor as far as the *ton* was concerned. In secret, only they would know the truth.

However, now that he saw her coming toward them, her gaze meeting first his, then Edmond's, he felt as if this was his wedding, as well. As she stood before them, he saw her happiness and realized he'd had a part in that. She was just as much his, and damn what society knew or did not know. She would always be his, too.

As Edmond spoke his vows to her, Colin met her gaze and hoped she saw in his eyes that he said them in his mind, and meant to uphold them. As she recited her vows, he noticed she took the time to look at them both, to show them that she held them equally in her heart. It was everything he could have asked for.

After a long ceremony and tedious wedding breakfast, he had retired to his newly purchased townhouse in Grosvenor Square— right next door to the newly wed Lord and Lady Ingham. As fate would have it, an old viscount who had grown weary of city life had decided to sell the place in order to retire to the country. The arrangement would benefit them all, putting him in close proximity while keeping up appearances.

It had already been established that they would split time between the two houses during the season, then spend their winters at Kesbridge, their summers in Bath or Brighton. No one would think it unusual if the bachelor friend of the earl spent his time in their home while not in London during the Season. It was the eternal fate of all bachelors to rely upon dinner invitations to eat many a night and the hospitality of others in order to escape boredom in the country, especially when one was not a first son with unlimited wealth at his disposal.

Though his new position with the War Office meant he was hardly hurting for money. Combined with his army half-pay, and money he'd wisely invested, he was well set.

Waiting for the day to come to an end so he could visit his bride had him on edge, and by the time the sun had gone down, he had to fight not to run next door and kick the door down. Taking his time, he left his own house through the servants' entrance, entering their garden by the back gate.

He was brought up short to find them waiting for him, Edmond in his shirtsleeves and waistcoat, Penelope in a simple pink gown, with her hair hanging down her back in soft waves.

She held Edmond's hand, but when she spotted him, she let go and ran forward to meet him. Colin reached for her, catching her up and lifting her against his chest. Their lips met, and he savored the moment, thoroughly tasting her before setting her back on her feet.

"I've missed you," she murmured, breathless from his kiss.

He kissed the tip of her nose and smiled. "And I you, my love. You did not have to wait for me. Leaving the door unlocked would have done."

"There's another bit of business we must attend to," Edmond said, coming forward to meet them. "And Penelope insisted it must be by moonlight."

He wrinkled his brow and glanced from Edmond to Penelope and back again. "What business?"

Clearing his throat, Edmond folded his hands before him and began intoning in his most solemn voice, "Dearlybeloved, we are gathered together here in the sight of God, and in the face of … well, in front of many flowers, to join together this man and this woman in holy matrimony…"

Colin frowned. "What the devil are you doing?"

Edmond grinned. "Marrying you and Penelope, naturally."

Taking his hands, Penelope smiled at him. "You stood up with Ed today, but we didn't get to make vows to each other. I want that for us, Colin. I want you to know that you have the same permanence in my life as Edmond."

Overcome by this gesture, particularly on Edmond's part, Colin felt his throat burning, his eyes stinging as if he might shed a tear. Clearing his own throat, he blinked it back and clasped Penelope's hands.

"I appreciate both of you for doing this for me."

"As Penelope's society husband, who better to marry you than me? Now then, shall we continue?"

Staring into Penelope's eyes, Colin saw her joy and experienced it as his own. "Yes, please."

Edmond continued on, leading them in the shorter version of a church wedding ceremony, complete with vows. Then, reaching into his pocket, he chuckled.

"Ah, I almost forgot. My wedding gift to you."

He produced two jeweler's boxes, glancing at their contents before handing them each one. Inside his was a woman's ring—a beautiful ruby set in gold and flanked by diamonds. The ruby was as large as the sapphire she already wore on her left ring finger. In Penelope's was what would appear like any man's ring to anyone who noticed him wearing it. However, he saw it for what Edmond intended it to be—a wedding band.

"Ed, you shouldn't have," he said.

His friend nodded, his jaw set in determination. "Like hell, I didn't. She's your wife, too, Colin. Now give her the bloody ring."

Chuckling, he removed the ring from the box, placing the little square into this pocket. Taking Penelope's right hand, he lifted it to his lips, kissing the knuckles.

"With this ring, I thee wed," he murmured, never breaking her gaze. "With my body, I thee worship, and with all my worldly goods, I thee endow: In the Name of the Father, and of the Son, and of the Holy Ghost. Amen."

Tears streaming down her cheeks, Penelope placed his ring on his right hand, and recited the same vow between sobs. Smiling, he cupped her face, wiping her tears away as Edmond pronounced them husband and wife.

He kissed her, understanding now that he'd needed this moment. That Edmond had thought to help in providing it showed him that he took Colin's place in Penelope's life as seriously as she did. With Penelope held against his side, he extended a hand to the best friend he'd ever had, the likes of which he knew he could never find again.

"Thank you."

Shaking his hand, Edmond shrugged. "I'm beginning to think that as Penelope's secret husband, you get all the perks. An intimate wedding without all the stiff formality, secret rings, clandestine walks through gardens in the middle of the night. Perhaps we went about this wrong."

Turning to him, she gave his chest a playful swat. "Quiet, you. It is too late to change things now. Nevertheless, no matter how things were planned, I could never have imagined it would be like this. Thank you both, for loving me the way you do."

Edmond frowned. "You don't need to thank us, darling. Love is love. You love us; we love you."

Shaking her head, she smiled. "But I do want to thank you. There was a time I thought love could not possibly be real. You both showed me how real it could be, and I am the most fortunate woman alive to have found it with not one man, but two."

Colin stroked a lock of her hair and kissed her forehead. "You're welcome, love."

"Now," she said with a coy smirk. "I can think of one benefit both my wonderful husbands get to take part in. And please, do so now before I die from anticipation."

Exchanging a glance with Edmond, Colin grinned. With a laugh, he reached for her, lifting and tossing her over his shoulder before darting through the garden toward the door with Edmond hot on his heels. The sounds of her laughter rung out through the dark garden.

EPILOGUE

SIX MONTHS LATER ...

*P*enelope inspected her reflection and smiled. The ball gown was one of the last pieces she'd had created before leaving London at the end of the Season. Emerald green silk set her hair on fire, the beaded bodice drawing the eye to the swell of her breasts—left quite exposed by her low neckline. The skirt hugged her hips before falling away in a flowing curtain of silk. Brilliant diamonds—a gift from her husbands—glittered around her neck and wrist. Perfect.

They had arrived at Kesbridge a fortnight ago, content to remain until Christmas, after which they would prepare to return to London. Though Colin might have to return before them alone. The War Office kept him quite busy, and Sir Henry Torrens had taken him firmly beneath his wing. A promotion in rank loomed on his horizon, and Penelope could not be more proud.

Meanwhile, Edmond continued to prove he was more than ready to step into the role of earl once his father had passed. The current earl still seemed to struggle with his gambling habit, though Penelope could see he tried his best to remain on the straight and narrow. Meanwhile, he had done the best thing for his family and the estate by placing Edmond in charge of managing the lands and income—which meant Penelope's dowry remained firmly in her legal husband's control, not her father-in-law's.

Under his diligence, the estate would flourish again, she felt sure of it. He worked hard each day, visiting the tenants to inquire about their needs. Every debt had been paid, all their accounts now in good standing.

Tonight, her mother-in-law was throwing a ball in her honor, a way to introduce the future countess to their neighbors. She looked forward to her first public ball with Edmond and Colin—who would be in attendance, as well. While they had to continue practicing discretion, Edmond's parents remained oblivious to the arrangement that existed between the three of them. Here in the country, the sprawling manor held plenty of far-flung wings and chambers where they could go to be together, blissfully undisturbed.

The sound of her dressing room door opening stole her attention, drawing her gaze. She found Edmond framed in the doorway, dressed in impeccable black and white evening attire. His gaze raked her from head to toe, his green irises darkening to emerald as they came to rest on her exposed bosom.

"You, are in big trouble, wife," he murmured, stepping into the room.

From behind him came Colin, drawing her admiring gaze in his scarlet dress uniform coat, his golden hair an overlong sweep of blond strands caressing his neck and forehead.

"Indeed, you are," he agreed, closing and locking the dressing room door behind him. "I do hope you have steeled yourself to receive your punishment."

Widening her eyes, Penelope played coy. "Whatever could I have done to deserve punishment?"

She backed away toward the bed, shivers wracking her as they began to stalk her like two jungle cats after a meal. Edmond began removing his coat, while Colin rounded to the other side of the bed.

Arching one eyebrow at her, Edmond chuckled. "Do you not recall leaving a pair of your drawers on my washstand, you little minx?"

Pressing one hand to her lips, she gasped. "Oh, dear. Is *that* where my drawers disappeared to? Heavens, I couldn't find them, so I simply opted to go without them this evening."

Having climbed up onto the bed after removing his coat, Colin grasped her from behind, lifting her up onto the mattress. Still removing his clothing, Edmond stood at the foot of the bed, watching as Colin yanked her up against his body, tilting her head for access to her neck.

"Yet another reason to punish her. Such a scandalous hussy, going about with no undergarments on. What a naughty girl you are, Penny."

She moaned when his lips and teeth found the side of her neck, nibbling on the straining tendons. He cupped her breasts, groaning in her ear as he discovered she went without a corset, as well.

"Nothing," Colin rasped. "She hasn't got a thing on under this gown."

Through his breeches, she could see Edmond's erection clearly outlined. "That does it. Something must be done. We simply cannot allow her to go to the ball looking like that. Every man in the room will be salivating to have her."

Pressing the length of his hard cock against her arse, Colin ground it against her, continuing on his path across her shoulder with his lips. She felt her gown loosening as he worked at the fastenings.

"No," Colin rasped, tearing at her clothes to get her out of them. "They can't have her. She's ours."

Unfastening his breeches, Edmond removed his final garment, causing a surge of moisture between her thighs at the sight of his cock, standing proudly beneath her hungry gaze. Realizing how the sight affected her, he grasped the organ in one hand and gave it a stroke, grinning when she whimpered and licked her lips.

"Shall we remind her who she belongs to?" he murmured, approaching the bed.

He plucked her from Colin's grasp, forcing her to her hands and knees before climbing on the bed with her, coming behind her. His hand caressed her spine, causing her to shiver. Grasping her hips, he smoothed his palms over her arse, his breathing growing ragged and harsh.

Pressing the head of his cock against her entrance, he teased her by entering her and withdrawing fully. She whimpered, swaying back into him, searching for what he kept from her. The sound of his hand cracking against her buttocks echoed along with her sharp cry from the room's high ceiling. Edmond caressed her flaming skin, leaving a soothing balm and a warmth that spread straight to her quim.

"Now, now," he murmured, pressing himself into her again. "Don't forget who is in control here. Are you in control, Penelope?"

Now undressed, Colin returned, kneeling in front of her, his erection straining toward her hungry mouth. She met his gaze, wiggling her hips again and taking Edmond in deeper.

He slapped her again, this time while Colin grasped the back of her neck and thrust toward her lips. She opened to take him in, moaning at the warmth, fading sting, and the smooth caress of Edmond's hand on her arse.

They showed her who was in control, who she belonged to without holding back—Edmond gripping her hips in a tight grasp as he began moving inside her so hard and fast, the sound of their bodies meeting created a rapid cadence in time with the swing of his heavy bollocks against her cunt, Colin fucking her mouth while his hands fondled her breasts, heightening her pleasure by tweaking her hard nipples. Screams burned in her throat, trapped by Colin's cock and the fact that she could hardly breathe through the intensity of her pleasure.

Edmond gave her another slap, harder this time, sending her crashing over the edge. Whimpering, she shuddered while her sheath captured him in a fist-tight hold, contracting around him in wild spasms. Grunting, he quickened his strokes, increasing the pleasure until she could bear no more and collapsed onto the bed. Colin withdrew from her, while Edmond lifted her.

She'd hardly caught her bearings before she realized Edmond had situated her on top of him. Entering her again, he grasped her hips and urged her to move, bouncing her up and down in his lap.

Hovering on the edge of a second climax, she braced her hands on his chest and rode him, waiting for Colin to join them for what had become her favorite way of being with them both. Nothing could compare to the way taking them both into her secret places felt, and she grew even wetter just thinking about it.

"Hurry, Colin!" she urged as he climbed over them, his body settling against hers while he positioned himself at her back passage. "I need you ... please."

Colin shuddered against her, his lips caressing her ear, shoulder, and neck as he slowly probed to enter her, as well. His cock, still wet from her mouth, forged a path through the tight ring of flesh offering entrance to her rear opening.

Becoming accustomed to making love this way had taken some getting used to, with both Edmond and Colin taking turns with her on alternating nights—allowing her to enjoy first one finger, then two, then eventually a cock invading the forbidden passage, introducing her to a new sort of pleasure. A pleasure she had always wondered about, and had come to enjoy as much as her husbands did. The first time they'd penetrated her at once, Penelope had enjoyed it so much that they endeavored to give her that same pleasure as often as she wanted—which proved to be nearly every time they made love.

Colin took his time, knowing he must ease his way in with her already filled with Edmond in one channel. Every time Edmond drew back, he gained an inch, until both of them moved back and forth inside of her, the pressure filling her, stretching her to the limit. They found a rhythm, one pulling out while the other thrust in—like a synchronized dance.

Holding on to Edmond, she laid her head back against Colin's shoulder and let them take her, her body overflowing with sensation, her heart near to bursting with love for them both. Beneath her, Edmond lifted his head, taking one of her breasts into his mouth, tickling the nipple with his tongue. Colin grasped her hip, his fingers sinking into her soft flesh, undoubtedly leaving fingerprints behind.

"I love you," he murmured, taking the shell of her ear between his teeth. "I love you, Penny."

Panting, she reached back to stroke his hair, her fingernails caressing the back of her neck. "And I love you, Colin. Always."

Turning her gaze to Edmond, she released Colin, reaching down to cup his face.

"And you," she moaned. "I love you, too, Edmond. Always."

Grasping her chin, he stroked her lower lip. Flicking out her tongue, she caressed the tip of his thumb, drawing a groan from deep in his chest.

"I love you," he replied. "Penny … our Penny. Say it. Tell us …"

He broke off on another moan, trembling as climax gripped him.

"Yours!" she cried as she and Colin followed Edmond closely, first her and then him. "I am yours!"

As they rose and spiraled over the edge together, Penelope knew they understood that she referred to both of them.

She collapsed onto Edmond, and Colin braced himself over her, though the tension melted from his body.

After a while, Colin slowly withdrew from her, then collapsed on the bed beside her and Edmond. Disengaging from Edmond, she lay between them, facing Colin, while Edmond wrapped his arms around her from behind. Colin's hand found her hair, stroking it as she burrowed her face against his chest.

"Well, I am certain it's safe to say we are late for the ball," Edmond murmured.

"Let them wait," Colin replied, lifting her chin to take her lips in a tender kiss. "I'm not ready to share her yet."

Edmond kissed the back of her neck, burying his face in her hair. "Hmm, me, neither."

She giggled. "Come, gentlemen, we must rise and dress. There will be plenty of time for more later."

Edmond groaned, and Colin sulked, but she managed to prod them from the bed. When she'd gathered her gown and slippers, Edmond laid her drawers and chemise over her arm, as well.

"Put them on, you little tease."

Appearing at his side, Colin held up her corset with a raised eyebrow. "Don't forget this. Else you'll need to be punished again."

Reaching out as she breezed past them, Edmond swatted her bare backside, sending her off with a stinging bottom.

As they dressed, she studied them from where she stood in the dressing room door, devouring them both with her eyes. Two perfect, beautiful men, both who belonged to her. How had she become so fortunate?

Making her way to the washstand, she quickly washed away the evidence of their encounter, then took up her 'forgotten' undergarments. As she dressed, her hands lingered over her belly, and she wondered when Edmond's seed would take root. Colin still continued to pull out of her to avoid impregnating her, while Edmond did everything he could to get her pregnant. The future earl required his heir, after all. Then, they'd decided, she would carry Colin's child. While it would carry Edmond's name, the three of them would always know the truth, and it would be enough for them.

A perfect, balanced family. Perhaps not by society's standards, but what did that matter? They were hers and she belonged fully to them both.

Besides, she'd quite decided whoever had come up with the number two when it came to love was a nitwit. It had become obvious to her that love was so much better experienced with three.

ABOUT THE AUTHOR

Sexy heroes ... sassy heroines ... electrifying erotic romance.
Victoria Vale has written over two dozen Romance and Young Adult
novels under various pseudonyms. As a lover of erotic romance, she
enjoys nothing more than a sexy hero paired with a sassy heroine,
flavored with a dash of spice and lots of heat. A wife and mother of
three, she enjoys reading (of course), cooking, sewing ... and other
activities that aren't appropriate for inclusion in a biography.